NIGHT OF THE LIVING MUMMY

R.L. STINE

SCHOLASTIC INC.

Goosebumps book series created by Parachute Press, Inc.
Copyright © 2024 by Scholastic Inc.

ISBN 978-1-339-01501-9

10 9 8 7 6 5 4 3 2 1   24 25 26 27 28

Printed in the U.S.A. 40
First printing 2024

PART ONE

Centerville Springs, Indiana

Present Day

1

HOW TO MUMMIFY A PERSON

I pointed to the three-pronged tool in the photo on my laptop screen. Kids in the back rows of the classroom leaned forward to see it better.

"This is what the ancient Egyptians used to pull the brain out of the skull," I said.

A few kids groaned. I heard my friend Jayden laugh. Jayden laughs at just about everything.

Mr. Horvat, our Science teacher, stepped in front of the laptop and studied the photo. "Happy, can you explain how the tool was used?" he asked.

I knew the answer. I know everything about ancient Egypt. It's not like I'm obsessed. I just have a thing about ancient Egypt. And mummies.

I actually dream about living in ancient Egypt and walking around the pyramids. And I dream about mummies. But the dreams aren't nightmares. Like, I'm not screaming and running because a mummy is staggering after me, trying to grab me.

My cousin Abby says it's easy to explain. She says it's because my mom is a paleontologist. That's a scientist who digs up ancient things like dinosaur bones. Abby says I dream about ancient Egypt because I want to be like my mom. Abby knows me pretty well. We see each other a lot because we're in the same class in school.

Jayden says I'm just weird.

He's probably right.

I pointed again to my laptop screen. "Here's what they did when they wanted to mummify someone," I said. "They slid this tool up the dead person's nose. They pushed it up until it reached the brain. Then they pulled the brain out through the nose."

Rena Graham in the front row made a loud gagging sound. She jumped up with a sick look on her face and ran out of the room, holding her hand over her mouth. Rena has a very sensitive stomach.

Other kids were groaning and moaning. Jayden was laughing.

"They had to clean out the body before they dipped it in burning tar," I said.

"Make him stop!" a kid in the back yelled.

Mr. Horvat stepped in front of the laptop before I could show the burning tar photo. "I think that's enough for now, Happy," he said. "Some of your classmates are feeling a little queasy." He chuckled. "I know *I* am." He burped into his hand.

"Mummifying someone was a difficult process," I said. "And pretty gross. I guess that's why a lot of people today are afraid of mummies."

"I think the movies about mummies coming to life are at fault," Mr. Horvat said. "Some of those movies are terrifying." He shivered.

"I *wish* mummies could come to life," I said. "Wouldn't it be awesome to actually talk to someone who lived in ancient Egypt?"

Of course, when I said that, I had no idea what a terrible wish that was.

BUILDING THE PYRAMID

After school, Abby and Jayden came home with me. I wanted them to help me finish the six-foot-tall LEGO pyramid I was building.

As we crossed through the living room, Abby picked up a few of the framed photos from the coffee table. "Don't you love all these baby pictures of Happy?" she said, holding them up to Jayden. "He has the same smile in every photo."

"Why do you think they call me Happy?" I said. "My mom says when I was born, I didn't cry. I came out smiling. She and Dad have called me Happy ever since."

"What's your *real* name?" Jayden asked. "Can you believe it? I totally forgot what it is."

"Harry," I said.

He laughed. "Harry Silverman? I like Happy a lot better."

"Happy is better than Grumpy or Dopey or Sneezy," Abby said.

Jayden and I squinted at her.

"Don't you know the names of the Seven Dwarves?" she asked.

Mom and Dad were at work. We helped ourselves to Cokes and chips and made our way up to my room to work on the pyramid.

I was building it in the center of the room. I had to push my bed against the wall to make space for it.

"I still can't believe all these yellow LEGOs," Jayden said. He's been helping me since I started it two months ago, and he says that every time.

"I wanted it to look like the bricks the Egyptians used," I said.

"But how do you buy thousands of yellow LEGOs?" Abby asked.

"It was expensive," I said. "Dad said he won't owe me any allowance for ten years."

The three of us dropped to our knees on the rug and began to add blocks to the pyramid.

"Guess you'll be up all night thinking about our class trip to the museum tomorrow," Jayden said.

"I'm totally pumped," I admitted. "I've been thinking about it nonstop."

"Why?" Abby asked. "We've been doing class trips to the City Center Museum downtown every year since second grade." She dropped a handful of blocks, and they clinked to the floor. "Oops. Sorry."

"But they just got their mummy this year," I said. "The first one ever. It's in the Egyptian Room. A real mummy. Not a replica."

"Guess you'll be going there first," Jayden said.

"If it's okay with Horvat," I replied. "I've been begging him to go there first for weeks."

Jayden shook his head. "I don't get it, Happy. It's just a totally gross old corpse wrapped up in smelly bandages."

"It's not just an ordinary corpse," I said. "It's an actual *king*. A king, Jayden. Who ruled all of Egypt."

Abby added a row of blocks to the side she was working on. "The last time I was in the Egyptian Room, I couldn't believe the jewelry. It was awesome. And it was so bright and sparkly. It looked brand-new."

"The Egyptians had a color blue that was very different," I said. "It had a special glow. But the recipe to make that dye was lost."

"I'll bet the Egyptians didn't have LEGOs this color!" Jayden said. Then he laughed at his own joke.

We worked on the pyramid till dinnertime. After we took photos of it to share online, Abby and Jayden stopped in the kitchen to say hi to my parents. Then they headed home.

"Hope you don't dream about mummies tonight!" Jayden called on his way out the front door.

"Hope I *do*!" I called back. And I did. But my dream that night was a nightmare.

I was walking by myself in the City Center Museum. Walking down a dark hall. I could hear my footsteps echo against the stone walls. I was lost. Where was the rest of my class?

I kept walking. The darkness was deep. I could barely see.

And something *grabbed* me.

I smelled it before I could see it. Even in the dream, I could smell its sour odor. And then its bandaged head came into view. And I knew a mummy had grabbed me.

It wrapped its ragged, moldy arms around my waist. And it whispered in my ear, a hoarse, rattling burst of air from deep in its chest.

"Run away. Run away while you still can."

7

DISASTER!

I woke up shivering in a cold sweat. I blinked at the shadows moving across my bedroom ceiling. *Just the shadow from the branches outside my window.* I tried to calm myself.

I waited for my heart to stop pounding in my chest. Then I got out of bed.

Why? I asked myself. *Why did I have a nightmare? I'm not afraid of mummies. I can't wait to see the one in the museum!*

I hurried to school. I was the first in line to board the yellow bus that was going to take us. It was a gray, rainy morning. I stood shivering in my rain poncho, waiting for the other kids to get in line.

Jayden came running up to me. He wore a big gray raincoat that came down below his knees. It didn't fit him at all. I guessed it was his dad's. His head looked lost inside the hood.

"I knew you'd be first in line, standing here in the rain," he said. "Afraid you'd miss the bus?"

Before I could answer, Abby bumped up behind us. "We could swim to the museum," she said.

"I'd swim there if I had to," I replied.

The bus doors opened. I climbed on and took a seat in the first row. Jayden kept walking. He always likes to sit in the middle of the bus. I don't know why.

Mr. Horvat followed everyone onto the bus. Water dripped from his rubber rain hat. He stood in the aisle using his fingers to count everyone. Then he raised a hand and waited for all of us to get quiet.

"We have one rule," he said. "Let's go through the museum together as a group. As you know, it's a large museum. I don't want people wandering off in all directions. It makes it too hard to keep track of you."

"Do we all have to go to the bathroom at the same time?" Rena Graham called out.

Everyone roared with laughter. Even Horvat. I think he laughed the loudest.

"I just want to be sure to bring most of you back with us," he said.

I think it was meant to be a joke. I heard Jayden laugh. I told you, he laughs at everything.

Mr. Horvat dropped into the empty seat next to me. He took off his hat and shook rainwater off it. "Nice morning for ducks," he said.

"I wonder if ducks really do like the rain," I replied. "I mean, I'll bet scientists have never really looked into it."

Horvat chuckled. "Happy, I like your brain."

I think he meant it as a compliment.

"I mainly made that announcement because of you," he said. We both bumped up from the seat as the bus jerked forward. "I know you've been begging me to run to the Egyptian Room first. But I'd really like you to wait for the rest of us."

"No problem," I said.

I *did* plan to run to the Egyptian Room first. But there was no point in sharing that information with him.

"We're going to start at the Colonial America wing," Horvat told me. "I know you've all been studying the colonies in your History class."

"Awesome," I said.

I hope the others all enjoy it, I thought. *I'll be close-up with an actual mummy.*

The bus pulled up to the front of the museum. Mr. Horvat stepped off, and I was the first to follow him.

The rain had slowed to a drizzle. I saw patches of blue sky over the roof of the museum. This was turning into the perfect day. I waited on the sidewalk as everyone climbed off the bus.

"Happy, see that?" Abby pointed to the top of the building.

I gazed up and saw the small rainbow she was looking at. "Rainbows are lucky," she said.

I knew this day was going to be awesome.

Jayden came off the bus last. "See the rainbow?" I said.

He looked up. But rain clouds had started drifting in, covering the blue sky again. He squinted at me. "You're seeing rainbows now? Do you need the nurse?"

I didn't answer him. I began trotting up the wide concrete stairs that led to the museum entrance.

Abby and Jayden were at my sides as we reached the top. "Want to ditch everyone and come to the Egyptian Room?" I asked them.

"No way," Abby said. "You heard Horvat."

"I'm sticking with the group," Jayden said. "If you're imagining rainbows, I don't want to be around you."

I rolled my eyes. "Great to have friends," I muttered.

"I don't have to be your friend," Abby said. "I'm your cousin."

A young woman in a dark business suit came hurrying up to meet us. She hugged a clipboard as she ran. Her blonde hair bounced behind her.

"Hi, people!" she shouted. "I'm Mary Stapleton. I'll be your guide for your visit. If you have any questions or problems, don't hesitate to ask me. I'm so happy to have your class here today."

Mr. Horvat stepped up to her, and they had a short conversation.

"Your teacher has made a good plan for you this morning," she announced. "Follow me to the right, and we'll begin in one of our best sections, the Colonial America wing."

Everyone went right. And I went left.

Of course, I knew where to find the Egyptian Room. I visited it every class trip. But this was the first time the room had an actual mummy.

I lowered my head and ran. I didn't look back.

The room was on the second floor. I didn't wait for the elevator. I raced up the stairs. I glanced back once. No one saw me.

My heart pounded as I reached the second-floor landing. My hands were suddenly ice-cold. I took a deep breath and turned into the hall that led to the exhibit.

"Whaaat?" I cried.

A thick rope stretched across the hallway.

I stopped and stared at it.

Why is this hall blocked off?

I grabbed the rope with both hands. I was about to lift it so I could climb under when a white-haired man in a dark blue uniform stepped out. His uniform cap was tilted over his head. A yellow badge on his jacket said: *SECURITY*.

I let go of the rope. "Can I get through here?" I asked.

"Sorry, kid. This section is closed," he said.

"But . . . I have to get to the Egyptian Room . . ." I said, gazing past him down the empty hall.

"Sorry," he repeated. "You can't go there today. The Egyptian Room is closed for repairs."

4

CAUGHT

"But—but—" I sputtered. "Is the mummy still there?"

He chuckled. "I don't think it went on vacation."

"Can I just see it? For one minute?" I asked. My voice came out high and shrill.

His smile faded. "No. Sorry. This whole wing is closed to museum visitors. The mummy isn't ready to greet his fans."

"But—I need to see him. I—"

"Some other day, kid," the guard said. "Trust me. You don't want to make this mummy angry."

I studied him. Was he trying to be funny? Or did he want to scare me?

We had a short staring contest. I knew he was waiting for me to turn around and walk away.

"Are you with anyone?" he asked finally. "Did your parents bring you?"

I shook my head. "No. I came with my class. From school."

"Maybe you should find them," he said.

"I guess," I murmured. I turned and started to walk away. I had my head down, my gaze on the floor. I was so disappointed, I thought I might cry.

But then I had an idea.

I remembered there was more than one way to get to the Egyptian Room. If I went up to the third floor and walked to the end of the hall, I could come back down on the other side of the museum.

Maybe there was no guard at the other end of the hall, and I could sneak into the room with no one seeing me. I only wanted to look at the mummy for a minute or two.

I had my phone in my back pocket. If I could just take a few photos . . .

When I reached the stairs, I glanced around. No one in sight. The guard wasn't following me.

I grabbed the railing and made my way quickly up to the third floor. On the third-floor landing, I peered back down. Still no one around.

The doors to this floor were closed. A sign above them read: DOLLHOUSES AND MINIATURES.

I pulled open a door and stepped inside. Loud voices rang in my ears. I squinted down the brightly lit hall. Two different groups of kids were huddled around glass display cases. A big day for school groups.

No problem, I thought. *I'll just walk past them. They won't pay any attention to me.*

I strode quickly and tried to look as if I belonged there. Before I reached the kids, I passed a long glass case of miniature trains. In another case, old-fashioned dolls, only a few inches tall, gazed out at me as I hurried past their shelves.

At the far end of the hall, a bunch of little kids were studying a shiny blue race car.

I headed to the first group of kids. They stood in a circle around a tall dollhouse in the middle of the floor. It was big enough for a person to climb inside. A young woman with a clipboard was describing it to them.

I froze when I heard a shout behind me.

"Hey, kid—stop!"

I spun around. The guard from downstairs! He was running hard, chasing after me, pointing his finger.

Caught. Too late to run.

I stopped and stood still to face him. My heart started to pound. He looked angry.

He was breathing hard by the time he got up to me. "I know what you're trying to do. You need to follow the rules," he said.

I shrugged. "I am," I replied.

"I told you to go back to your class," he said. He pointed to the kids around the dollhouse. "Is this your class?"

"Y-yes," I lied. "It's my class."

He turned to the young woman with the clipboard. "Is this guy in your class?"

She wrinkled her forehead as she squinted at me. "I've never seen him before," she said.

GRABBED

"Oh. Sorry," I said. "That's my class over there." I pointed to the group of kids admiring the race car at the other end of the hall.

The guard frowned. I don't think he believed me.

I turned and started to trot over to the other class. As I ran, I raised my hand and waved at them.

Two of the kids waved back.

The guard probably figured that I knew them. I glanced behind me and saw him walking the other way.

Whew. I didn't know I was such a good liar.

I sprinted past the race car and the class and kept going. My heart was still pounding as I made it to the double doors at the far wall. I pushed a door open and stepped out to the landing. Then I grabbed the banister and crept back down to the second floor.

I expected to see a rope across this end of the hall. But no.

I listened for footsteps. No security guard on this side. I took a few more steps. I could see the entrance doors to the Egyptian Room . . . Close . . . So close.

I'm going to make it, I thought. *There's no one on this side of the building to stop me.*

But before I could move, gray arms wrapped around me from behind. I saw them before I felt them. They wrapped around my waist and tightened. Held me . . . held me in place.

The mummy!

I let out a shrill scream that rang down the long hall.

SOMETHING SCARY IN THE EGYPTIAN ROOM

"Gotcha!" a voice rasped in my ear. "Gotcha!"

"Whoa." I shook my body hard, twisted, and broke free from the arms holding me. With a gasp, I staggered away. Spun around.

And stared at Jayden, who was laughing hard.

Jayden in the big gray raincoat with the sleeves that were way too long for him.

Not the mummy. Jayden. Laughing with tears in his eyes, enjoying his joke.

"What is your *problem*?" I screamed. I punched him hard in the shoulder.

That made him laugh even harder. "I knew I'd find you here," he said.

I still had my fist raised, ready to punch him again. "You scared me to death," I growled.

"When I saw the rope down at the other end and

the security guard, I knew where I'd find you," Jayden said. "Trying to sneak into the Egyptian Room from this side."

I lowered my fist and turned toward the entrance. "Well, good for you," I said. "So now you're a mind reader."

"Horvat sent me to get you," Jayden said. "He finally noticed you were gone. We're going to see the armor and swords and weapons next. He doesn't want you to miss it. It's pretty awesome."

I didn't say anything.

"Are you coming with me?" Jayden asked.

"No," I said. "I'm going in there." I pointed to the Egyptian Room. "I'm going to take a short video and some photos. Then I'll come downstairs."

"But if you get caught—" Jayden started.

I started to the doors. "If I hurry, I won't get caught. Do you want to come?"

"No way," he answered. "No way I'm getting in trouble just to look at a moldy old pile of bandages."

He tried to pull my arm, but I swiped it away from him. "Come on, Happy," he said. "We can come back and see the mummy some other day."

"Catch you later," I said. I pulled open the door to the Egyptian Room and stepped inside.

I was greeted by a blast of hot air. The room was dark. A rectangle of orange sunlight washed in from a window in the far wall. A sharp odor made me sneeze. Cleaning fluid?

I kept blinking till my eyes adjusted to the darkness. My heart was pounding like a bass drum. I glanced around. The area was actually divided into three large rooms.

I stood there frozen, like a statue. I held my breath and tried to calm myself down.

The nearest room had a tall model of a pyramid. I could see large photos taken recently of the pyramids near Cairo on one wall.

I forced myself to move to the room beside it. I peered into the gray light. I saw display shelves of ancient Egyptian pottery and tools and several shelves of Egyptian jewelry.

That meant the mummy was in the third room. I hesitated at the open doorway. Then I burst inside.

Yes. The stone mummy case rested on its back in the center of the room.

My legs felt weak as I walked toward it. I had to force myself to breathe. The mummy case was open.

This is actually happening, I told myself. *I'm about to see a five-thousand-year-old mummy.*

A sign on the wall behind the mummy case caught my eye. I stepped up to it and squinted at the words: MUMMIFIED REMAINS OF RAMAN THE BOY KING. APPROX. 5,000 BCE.

A boy? He died when he was a boy?

I tried to picture a boy my age—twelve—in a king's robe and crown. I saw him sitting on a throne, surrounded by his followers and servants, all in colorful robes.

How did Raman die?

I spun to the case. Gripped the stone sides with both hands. And gazed down at the mummy.

"Wow!" A cry escaped my lips.

He was so small. Smaller than me. Stretched out on his back, his arms crossed over his narrow chest. He was only about four feet tall.

His bandaged head was smooth and shaped like a light bulb. The bandages over his body were stained brown and black. The ancient tar had turned as gray as stone.

Leaning closer, I could see two ruts where his eyes had been. Cloth strips on his right shoulder hung loose.

One of his bandaged hands was closed in a fist. The other hand lay open on his chest.

"Whoa. Whoa." Was I about to faint from excitement?

Gripping the side of the mummy case, I leaned even closer. I wanted to smell the mummy. I wanted to smell the ancient aroma of tar and cloth.

I lowered my head slowly . . . lowered it close to the mummy's bandaged body.

And let out a horrified scream as the mummy sat up and turned to face me.

7

"WHAT IS HAPPENING TO ME?"

"No!" I screamed. "Noooo!"

My hands still gripped the stone side of the case. I staggered back and stumbled against the wall.

The mummy stretched his arms above his head, a long stretch. His sour odor washed over me.

I pressed my back against the wall. I started to choke. I couldn't breathe.

The mummy leaned forward, then back, as if testing itself. Its bandaged head turned again to face me.

Could it see me?

This couldn't be happening. Mummies come alive only in movies or in dreams.

But I'm not dreaming this. I'm wide awake.

I opened my mouth to scream for help. But no sound came out.

"Come closer." The whispered words sent chills down my body.

"You—you can speak!" I choked out.

"Come closer," it repeated in a raspy croak.

"N-no!" I stammered, pressing myself harder against the wall.

I knew I should be excited. This was amazing. A dream come true.

But it was too frightening. Too terrifying.

The ancient Boy King raised a hand and beckoned to me.

"Noooo!" I cried out again.

And then I felt a strong push—as if someone was shoving me away from the wall. I stumbled forward.

The mummy beckoned again.

And, again, I felt the heavy force behind me. Pushing me . . . pushing me to the mummy case.

I tried to fight it. But I wasn't strong enough.

The mummy beckoned one more time.

Squeezing my hands against the stone side of the case now, I tried to push myself away. But I couldn't move.

The strong force pulled me down . . . pulled me . . . pulled me over the side of the coffin.

My head filled with a loud buzzing that made me gasp. I felt dizzy . . . too weak to fight back . . . the buzzing grew louder . . . deafening . . .

I struggled to stand up. But powerful vibrations running through my body kept me from moving.

And now I was face-to-face with the mummy.

Nose to nose.

I felt the scratch of the ancient cloth as my head pressed against the bandaged face . . . pressed . . . pressed . . .

I smelled the ancient odor of death. I felt the bandages wrap around me . . . felt the hard dry tar against my skin. Felt myself sinking . . . sinking into the throbbing darkness.

What is happening to me?

PART TWO

Ancient Egypt

Thousands of Years Ago

THE BOY KING

Raman swept his purple robe around him as he entered the throne room. The chamber was crowded with people who jumped up from their seats on the floor and stood stiffly, watching him as he made his way to the golden throne.

Raman used the royal scepter as a walking stick. He liked the *clonk, clonk, clonk* it made as he tapped it in front of him on the marble floor.

His purple sandals felt tight as he stepped across the chamber.

I'm still growing, he thought. *I am king, but I haven't reached my full height.*

The thought struck him funny and made him sad at the same time. Raman knew the reason: He was envious of Akila, his little sister, and Omari, his younger brother.

They got to play in the nursery chamber. Carefree. They could play Hounds and Jackals and Twenty Squares and all the other board games for hours. And play with the cats, and chase each other through the palace. And prance and dance in the sand at the shore and be as free as the geese that floated down the river.

Ever since the day his father had died in battle, Raman had the weight of the kingdom on his shoulders.

Isis, his mother, named after the goddess of healing and magic, walked behind him. She tapped him on the shoulder as he began to lower himself onto his throne.

"You may be our glorious king," she said, "brighter than the sun and all that. But you still need to learn some manners."

"Sorry, Mother." Raman stepped down and allowed his mother to take her throne first. Isis sat on his right. Raman waited for Khufu, his royal advisor, to take his place on the throne to Raman's left.

Khufu was older than the pyramids, at least in Raman's eyes. He had advised Raman's father. And now Raman couldn't make a decision or say a word without Khufu offering his wisdom and advice.

He thinks he's king, Raman often thought. *Since when does being old make you wise? Since when does it make you king?*

Khufu leaned close. His bristly white beard scratched Raman's cheek. Raman smelled fish on Khufu's breath.

"You must be tough with these followers," he rasped in Raman's ear. "They see you as a boy. So they expect you to be soft. Show them the strength of a king."

Raman nodded but didn't reply.

What if I don't want to be a tough judge? What if I'd rather be a kind judge?

The people crowded the throne room to ask their king for help. And to settle their disputes.

"Let's begin," Khufu said, sending another cloud of fish breath into Raman's face. "Show them the power of the throne."

I'd rather show them how fair I can be, Raman thought.

Raman rubbed his hand over the gold amulet he wore on a chain around his neck. The amulet portrayed the god Osiris. Tutanak, Raman's father, had warned his son never to take it off.

"The amulet holds powerful magic," Tutanak had told him. "Magic over the sands and the seas. Magic that can defeat any enemy. Don't ever lose control of it, or it could mean doom for all of us."

He placed the amulet around Raman's neck a few

moments before he died. Raman had worn it ever since. He hadn't dared to explore its magic. But he remembered his father's warning.

Raman was always squeezing it, rubbing his hand over it, making sure it was in place on his chest. At night, he prayed to Osiris to make him worthy of such powerful magic.

Khufu waved his hand, and the first palace visitors stood and approached the throne. Two long-haired young men in modest gray robes bowed their heads to Raman and awaited permission to speak.

Khufu waved his hand again. "What matter do you bring to the king?" he demanded.

"This man has taken a camel that doesn't belong to him." The first man spoke. "I have not come here to have him punished. I just want the camel returned to me."

Raman turned to the other young man and waited for him to give his side.

"The camel was born on my land," the man said. "This man's animals feed on my land. The camels are with me for days, and he makes no attempt to take them away. He—"

"But they are still my property," the first man interrupted.

"He makes no attempt to pay me or thank me in any way," the second man said. "So I have taken one camel as payment. I believe it is my due."

The first man opened his mouth to argue. But Khufu grabbed Raman's scepter and raised it high to silence them both.

Khufu leaned into Raman. "You are king of Egypt," he rasped. "You have the light of the sun god and the power of the Nile. These men insult you by bringing a dispute about a lowly camel to your palace."

"They came because they need a judgment," Raman said. "I must—"

"They should both be put to death," Khufu rattled in Raman's ear. He squeezed the sleeve of Raman's robe. "Tell them they will be put to death for bringing such an insult to the Pharaoh of Egypt."

"No!" Raman cried. He jerked free from Khufu and leaned away from him. "No. That is too harsh."

"You must be harsh," Khufu insisted. Behind his white beard, his face reddened. "You must show them you are not a boy."

Raman raised his eyes to the two young men. They stood in silence, watching the argument between the king and his elderly advisor.

Raman thought hard. *How shall I settle this dispute?*

Again, Khufu leaned his body against Raman and brought his face close to Raman's ear. "If you don't like my first advice," he rattled, "tell them to bring the camel to the palace, and it will be put to death. That will settle the problem for good and teach them not to waste the king's time."

If only Khufu were a camel! Raman thought. The idea made him laugh.

Raman took his scepter from Khufu's hand. He tapped it loudly on the floor. Then he turned to the two men.

"You may take back your camel," he told the first man. "The camel is yours. In return, you will pay your friend here two cubits of grain."

"But my land is small," the first man argued. "Two cubits—"

"Two cubits of grain," Raman repeated. He tapped the scepter again twice.

The men bowed their heads to the king. Then they turned and walked away, disappearing into the crowd.

Khufu shook his head unhappily. His face was still a deep scarlet. "Weak," he muttered to Raman. He waved his hand to summon the next visitor.

The morning went slowly for Raman. He listened to every complaint and argument. He wanted to give his best advice, his wisest ruling.

In each case, Khufu's suggestion was harsh and merciless. It seemed that the old advisor hated the people who came to see the king. He wanted to see them die. He wanted them punished.

Did he want them to hate Raman? To see Raman as a cruel leader?

After two hours, Raman turned to Isis, his mother. "Enough for now," he said. "Let us eat our afternoon meal."

He let Isis rise first, then started to follow her out of the throne room.

Khufu stopped him at the doorway. "Raman, you may be king," he said, "but I have the *wisdom* of a king."

Raman didn't know how to reply to that. He swept his robe around him and strode past Khufu.

Raman had no idea that he would never sit on the throne again.

THE KING IS ATTACKED

Raman started to follow his mother to her chamber. He let out a cry when someone pushed him hard from behind.

Stumbling, he crashed into Isis. She spun around and grabbed his shoulders to steady him.

"Omari, why did you shove me?" Raman cried to his grinning little brother.

Omari shrugged. His dark eyes flashed. "I just felt like it." Omari was the baby in the family. He knew he would be forgiven for anything.

Isis bent down and straightened the front of Omari's robe. She couldn't help but smile at her youngest child. "Do you think it's proper to attack the king?" she asked.

"He doesn't look like a king to me," Omari answered. "He looks like Raman."

Raman pinched his brother's nose.

Omari slapped Raman's hand away. "Why did you do that?"

Raman laughed. "I just felt like it."

Omari grabbed the scepter from Raman's hand and stood it up straight in front of him. "Can I be king now, too?" he asked.

Raman and Isis laughed. Omari could always make them laugh.

"Why do you want to be king?" Isis asked.

"Because then I could make Raman come play Twenty Squares with Akila and me."

Raman shook his head. "I told you before. I won't play with Akila and you because you cheat."

"We do not!"

"Then why don't I ever win?" Raman demanded. "Why do I lose every game?"

Omari laughed. "Because you're a bad player."

Isis took the scepter from Omari and handed it back to Raman. "Go back to your sister," she told Omari. "Raman and I need to talk."

The little boy's shoulders slumped. "So I can't be king?"

"You can't be king while I am king," Raman told him.

"Can I be king when you *die*?"

Isis gasped. "Omari, what a *horrible* thing to say!" she cried.

Raman stared open-mouthed at his brother.

"Apologize to Raman," Isis ordered.

Omari didn't apologize. He stood there grinning. Then he spun away and went running toward the nursery. When he was almost out of sight, he called back, "Sorry!"

Shaking his head, Raman followed his mother into her chamber. The room was draped in cloth of violet and deep red.

Raman sat beside Isis on a carved wooden bench. Servants brought them water in goblets of gold. "What do you wish to speak to me about?" Raman asked.

"Khufu," his mother answered. "I could see your growing impatience with him in the throne room."

"Can I send him away?" Raman demanded. "I don't want him leaning over me, breathing his fish breath and bad advice in my ear." He shuddered. "I can still feel the bristle of his whiskers scraping my face when he talks to me."

"Perhaps you can learn something from him," Isis said. "He was your father's trusted advisor, and—"

"Learn something from him?" Raman jumped to

40

his feet. "Khufu only wants to punish everyone. Punish them or kill them. His advice isn't wise. He is a bitter old man who—"

"I believe he is trying to help you," Isis said. "He wants you to appear strong. People see that you are a boy. If you don't act like a man, people will not accept you as the king of Egypt."

"But I *am* the king!" Raman cried. "Khufu thinks he is king. And he—he—" He gripped the amulet that swung in front of his chest. "If only I could use the magic of this amulet and send Khufu to another land."

Isis raised a hand to silence him. "Let go of the amulet, my son. Do not think about its magic. The magic of Osiris is not for someone of your age."

"But—but—" Raman sputtered.

"Can I ask you to be patient? Patience is a kingly quality. You may not agree at all times with Khufu—"

"I *never* agree with him!" Raman shouted.

Isis kept her hand raised. "Patience," she repeated. "Patience . . ."

Raman was still thinking about Khufu when he went to bed that night. Two servants wrapped him in his sleeping robes. Another servant pulled the silken covers over

41

him when he lowered himself into his bed.

He shut his eyes and pictured himself raising the amulet in both hands. He imagined calling up the powers of Osiris. Then he saw Khufu, flying through the air.

Khufu, his robe sailing above his head as he flew, helplessly waving his arms like a bird. Khufu flying high above the world, flying endlessly, flying forever.

Khufu sailing to the end of the earth, far away from everyone. Far away from Raman and the throne room.

Eyes shut, Raman pictured this. And the fantasy brought a smile to his face as he drifted into sleep.

A short while later, a sharp pain in his stomach made him wake up, screaming.

He tried to sit up, but a heavy weight pressed him into the bed.

Darkness all around. Too dark to see.

Hands punched at his face. A body bounced on him. Pounded him.

He screamed again. Screamed to his servants, "Attack! Help me! I am attacked in my bed!"

MISSING

Light flickered in the chamber entrance as his servants rushed in, holding flaming torches in front of them.

Raman struggled to raise himself. But his attackers held him to the bed.

Light washed over him—and he stared at his brother and sister. Bouncing on him. Punching him. Wrapping him in the bed sheets.

"Omari! Akila!" he screamed. "Get off me! Get off!"

The kids giggled as they pounced on him. Akila tugged at his long, dark hair. Omari began to tickle his stomach.

The servants stopped and held their torches high. The firelight appeared to dance over the kids as they enjoyed their surprise attack. Seeing there was no serious trouble, the servants left the chamber.

Raman finally managed to pull himself up to a sitting position. He pushed Akila away and grabbed Omari's hands, forcing the tickling to stop.

"What is the meaning of this?" Raman cried. "What are you two doing in here?"

"We couldn't sleep," Akila said. She swept her long curls behind her shoulders.

"You couldn't sleep so you decided to hurt me?" Raman said.

They both nodded.

Raman narrowed his eyes at them. "Whose idea was it?" he demanded.

Akila pointed to Omari. Omari pointed to Akila. They both laughed.

Raman laughed, too. He pulled them both into a hug.

After a few seconds, he lowered his arms. He climbed to his feet and raised a hand to his chest.

The amulet.

He rubbed his hand over his chest. He swept back the bedcovers and peered at the bed. He felt for the chain around his neck. He swiped at his chest again as cold panic gripped him.

The amulet.

It was gone.

11

DEATH IN THE PALACE

Akila didn't see Raman's panic. She began jumping up and down on his bed.

Omari reached to tickle his big brother again. But Raman pushed him away. "My amulet," Raman said, searching the bedclothes again. "Have you seen it?"

Omari giggled. Gripping the front of his robe, he turned away from Raman.

"Why are you laughing?" Raman demanded. "Have you seen it?"

Omari stood with his back to Raman. He giggled again.

"Have you?" Raman cried. He spun his little brother around and pulled open his robe.

And stared at the gold amulet hanging from Omari's neck.

"You thief!" Raman cried. He burst out laughing, so happy the amulet hadn't been stolen.

He lifted it from Omari's neck and lowered it over

his own head. Then he smoothed the cool metal over his chest. His heart had been racing, but now it slowed, and he began to feel normal.

"The amulet has the magic of Osiris," he told his little brother. "Too powerful for you."

"I like magic," Akila said, still standing on the bed.

"Then I have a magic trick for you," Raman told them. "Let's see if you can make yourself disappear."

He lifted Akila off the bed. Then he gave them both gentle shoves toward the bedchamber door.

It took Raman a long time to fall back to sleep. He kept thinking about the amulet and being king, the leader of so many people. The amulet suddenly felt heavy on his chest.

Was he ready to be king? Was he wise enough?

He thought about Khufu and his cruelty. Should he stop fighting and listen to the old man's advice?

He was still thinking about these things the next day when Khufu joined Raman and his mother for their late-day meal. Servants scurried around the long table, carrying all sizes of platters and bowls.

"Your favorite today," Isis said to her son as a servant placed a bowl before him. "The oxen stew has been prepared just for you."

Raman tore off a hunk of bread and dipped it into

the steaming, dark stew. "Very good." He wiped his lips and reached for his goblet, filled with goat's milk.

The servants filled the other two goblets with beer. The beer was thick and tasted sweet. Everyone drank it for the nourishment and for good health.

The three of them raised their goblets in a toast. "To Raman the Boy King," Khufu said.

The next part of the meal was served. Raman looked down into the large bowl of dates, figs, cucumbers, and melon slices.

"How will you spend the afternoon?" Isis asked him.

Raman turned to answer her. But he saw something leap up from the large bowl. Before he could move, his throat exploded in a burst of sharp pain. Roaring in shock, he staggered to his feet.

Something gripped his throat.

Isis and Khufu both uttered cries of horror.

A snake. A fat black snake, wriggling as it pierced Raman's skin.

Isis and Khufu screamed, screamed to the servants for help.

Raman gripped the snake in one hand and tried to tug it away. But the creature had buried its teeth deep into his throat.

47

Raman jerked and pulled the snake. But it only sent more shockwaves of pain coursing through his body. He twisted and squirmed and tugged. But the teeth were planted too deep in his neck.

"Khufu, do something!" Isis cried out. "Help him! Help my son!"

But Khufu remained frozen.

Raman felt himself weakening. The light faded. He dropped to the floor. Trapped inside the pain, his body folded on itself.

And then he lay flat behind the table and didn't move.

His eyes wide with horror, Khufu finally sprang from his seat. He dropped to his knees beside Raman. He placed a hand on the boy's neck.

A servant grabbed the snake, jerked it away in both hands, and ran off with it.

Khufu raised his eyes to Isis. "He—he's dead," he stammered. "The Boy King is dead."

12

CAN HE BE REVIVED?

"Someone murdered my son," Isis said. Tears ran down her flushed cheeks. Arms tightly crossed in front of her, she paced back and forth in Raman's bedchamber.

Shaking their heads in disbelief, servants stood silently against the wall.

Draped in red silk, the boy's body had been placed on its back on the bed. His eyes had been shut. His arms crossed over his chest.

Isis tore at her hair with both hands and uttered sob after sob. She stopped when Khufu came striding into the room.

"The serpent has been killed," he said, breathing hard. "And the chef and the servant who placed the bowl in front of him have also been put to death."

Isis scowled at the old man. "That will not bring back my son."

"Justice for this crime will be done," Khufu told her. "Egypt is without a king."

"I am without my beautiful son!" Isis wailed.

"Since Omari is too young to take the throne," Khufu said, "I am prepared to assume the duties of the king."

Isis stared at him but didn't reply.

"But that might not be necessary," Khufu went on. "I have sent for Vathor."

"Vathor." Isis repeated his name. "Does that old sorcerer have the power to bring Raman back from the dead? They say his powers have weakened."

Khufu rubbed his beard with one hand. He nodded. "If anyone has the power to bring our king back to life, it is Vathor."

"I have heard stories that he is a great wizard," Isis said.

"Vathor used his powers to end the seven-year famine," Khufu told her. "The wheat crops grew back under his powers. And he found the magic to cure Nile fever when our young people's skin erupted in black blotches."

Isis and Khufu turned and gazed at Raman's lifeless body. The tears began to roll down Isis's cheeks again. "If only Vathor's magic will work today," she murmured.

"Raman will breathe again," Khufu said. "The great wizard will not fail us."

A buzzing fly landed on Raman's forehead. Khufu hurried to brush it away.

Vathor walked slowly, bent over. His long, pointed white beard nearly touched his knees. His black robe swept over the floor as he made his way across Raman's bedchamber.

"Welcome, Vathor," Khufu said, stretching his arms out to the ancient sorcerer. "Your powers are needed today."

Vathor bowed deeply and nearly toppled over.

"Only you can breathe life into our murdered Boy King," Khufu said. He followed the wizard to the side of the bed.

Vathor bent over the boy's body. "What caused the wound at his throat?" he asked. His voice was a shrill whistle. "Is that a snakebite?"

Khufu nodded. "Yes. The venom of a snake has killed the Boy King."

"Can you bring him back to us?" Isis demanded in a trembling voice. She grabbed the shoulder of the wizard's robe. "Can you? Can you do it?"

Vathor pressed his hand on the dried wound. Then he smoothed Raman's neck with his wrinkled hands.

He turned to Isis and Khufu. "The king will live again," he said. "You will see—his face will be bright as the sun, his voice as lilting as the songbirds that grace the trees in springtime."

Isis groaned. "Vathor, please save the poetry for after my son is returned to us."

Vathor nodded. He reached into the deep pocket of his robe. He pulled out a small gray bottle.

"Stand back," he told Isis and Khufu. "This powder is poison to all who are alive. But a tonic to the dead."

Isis and Khufu stepped away. Against the bed-chamber wall, servants murmured to one another and watched wide-eyed.

The old wizard poked a finger and thumb into the gray bottle. Then he lifted them out and sprinkled a sparkling blue powder over Raman's face. He reached into the bottle a second time and sent another shower of powdery blue flakes over the boy's head.

Muttering chants filled with words Isis and Khufu had never heard, Vathor pulled another bottle from his robe. He pinched a small wad of a red powder between his fingers. Then he rubbed the powder over Raman's throat wound.

For a long moment, he leaned over the boy's body, pressing the red powder on the throat, muttering more strange words to himself.

Finally, he straightened up, backed away from the bed, and turned to Isis and Khufu.

"Success?" Isis demanded, her voice trembling and weak. "Have you done it?" She clasped her hands together in a praying position.

The old wizard bowed to her. "The Boy King will sit up and breathe when I command it," he said.

Bent nearly in half, he took a few more steps back. Then he pushed up the sleeves of his robe. He raised both hands above his head.

And he shouted in his high, whistle of a voice: "Rise, Boy King! Rise now—and live."

All eyes in the room were on Raman's body. No one breathed. No one made a sound.

Raman didn't move.

Vathor still held his hands above his head. "Arise, Raman!" he shouted. "Arise now! I command you to sit up and breathe!"

Raman's body remained still.

Vathor lifted his gaze to the ceiling and let out a long whoosh of air. He stepped closer to the body on the bed.

"Arise now!" he shouted at the top of his lungs. "Arise now, oh Boy King!"

Silence in the large chamber. No one dared utter a sound.

And then Khufu's whisper broke the silence. "Look—did he move? Did Raman move?"

13

WHERE IS THE AMULET?

Isis clapped her hands to her cheeks. Some of the servants gasped and uttered cries.

Vathor stepped back, eyes focused on the body on the bed, hands still raised above his head. "Arise . . . arise . . . arise," he repeated in a whisper.

But the body did not move. Raman did not sit up. Raman did not breathe. The dead Boy King didn't twitch or move even the width of a finger.

A heavy silence fell over the chamber. With a sigh, Vathor finally brought his arms down to his sides. He lowered his head and turned away from Isis and Khufu, as if ashamed.

Isis and Khufu stood stiffly, staring at the boy's body, afraid to speak, praying that Vathor's spell would take hold. They waited . . . waited . . . until Isis could bear it no longer. She burst into loud sobs, spun away, and went running from the bedchamber.

55

The old wizard buried his face in his robe. "I have failed," he choked out. "My powers have failed me, Khufu." He started to the doorway. "Let me leave to go live with my shame."

Khufu watched the bent old man hobble out. Then he turned to the servants against the wall. "Raman will be mummified and set to rest with all the glory of a king of Egypt!" he exclaimed. "Prepare the body!"

The mummification ceremony was held in the Great Hall. Thousands of robed followers crowded the vast chamber, eager to see their lost king. After the ceremony, the mummy would be locked forever in the tomb known as the Pyramid of the Kings.

Priests chanted prayers as the boiling tar was poured over the Boy King's body. The prayers continued as the wide strips of cloth were wrapped around him until the tar was covered.

Isis sat with Omari and Akila in the royal grandstand behind the priests. For once, the brother and sister were still, their faces solemn. They realized they were saying goodbye forever to their older brother.

Isis wept openly, her cries drowned out by the priests' chanting. Many others in the vast chamber cried, too, sobbing loudly. A dark moment in their lives and in their history.

As king, Khufu stood beside the mummification table. He insisted on instructing the priests, even though they knew their jobs well.

When the bandages were thick around Raman's body, covering it from head to foot, the priests stopped their work. They turned to the crowd of onlookers and began to sing.

Everyone stood and began to sing a dark, mournful song of farewell. The roar of voices rang like thunder off the chamber walls. This song was followed by a joyful song, a song of hope and promise for the future of the kingdom.

When it ended, the crowd stood in place and didn't leave. They watched in silence as servants carried the mummy of Raman from the chamber. They were followed by Khufu and Isis, Omari and Akila, and other members of the royal family.

The mummy was carried to its tomb inside the Pyramid of the Kings. Then it was lowered into the stone case where it would rest forever. The mummy was placed on its back. Its arms were crossed over its chest.

More chants were sung by the priests. Isis and the

others bowed their heads and waited for them to finish.

The final moment had arrived. The moment when ten servants would lift the heavy stone lid of the case and cover Raman beneath it. The servants moved to lift the case—

—when Isis screamed for them to stop.

"Stop! Stop right now! STOP!" She burst from Khufu and her children, dove forward, and blocked their way.

"The amulet!" Isis screamed. "Raman must be buried with the amulet of Osiris!" Breathing hard, she peered at all those around her. Her gaze landed on Khufu.

"The amulet! Where is it?" she demanded. "The amulet is MISSING!"

14

A SHOCK IN THE TOMB

Two days later, Khufu came to Isis's chamber. "I've come to report to you . . ." he said.

Isis sat at a mirror while servants braided her hair. She waved the servants away and turned to Khufu. "To report to me that you have found the amulet?" she said.

Khufu shook his head. His scraggly white hair shook with it. He avoided her eyes. "We have failed to find it."

"You must keep searching," Isis ordered.

"We have searched every chamber," Khufu said. He gazed down at the floor. "For two days. The amulet was not found in Raman's bedchamber. Or in the Great Hall. Or in the nursery. Or in the dining hall. Or in any rooms Raman might have visited."

"Then it was stolen," Isis said. She shuddered. "Stolen by an enemy of the kingdom."

"Perhaps—" Khufu began.

"We cannot rest while some thief has the power of

Osiris in his hands," Isis said. And then another thought flashed into her mind. "Was Raman murdered for the amulet's magical powers? Was he murdered by the amulet's thief?"

Khufu opened his mouth but didn't speak.

Isis narrowed her eyes at him. "Of course, my wise old advisor, the suspicion falls on *you* first."

"Me?" Khufu cried. He took a stumbling step backward. "Me? N-no!" he sputtered. "I have been loyal to your family my whole life. Why would I—?"

"To be king," Isis said, pointing a finger at him. "You murdered Raman to make yourself king. Once my boy was dead, it was easy for you to steal the amulet and—"

"Stop!" Khufu shouted. He raised both hands in front of his face. "Stop! I will not listen to this. You must calm yourself. You are thinking wild thoughts."

Khufu's face was bright red. His eyes bulged nearly out of his head. "I am a loyal servant. I may have been harsh with Raman. But I loved the boy as if he were my own."

He bowed to her. "Isis, you may take my life if you do not believe me. You can have me put to death if you doubt my loyalty."

She let out a sigh. "Very well," she said. "I will

believe you. But who is the villain who murdered my son and stole the amulet?"

"Perhaps the amulet was not stolen," Khufu said. "Perhaps it was just misplaced."

Isis narrowed her eyes at him. "What do you mean?"

"Let us return to Raman's tomb," the old advisor said. "Let us search the case where he rests one more time. Perhaps the amulet fell into the case while he was being placed in it."

Isis gazed at him. Was this a desperate last hope?

"We must try everything," she said finally. "I will summon the servants to take us to the tomb."

They traveled in a draped carriage carried on the shoulders of eight servants. The afternoon sunlight washed over them. But the high entrance to the pyramid tomb rose up dark as night.

Their footsteps echoed in the stone passageways. The tomb of the Boy King stood hidden deep in the pyramid where no intruders could find it.

Far in the distance, Isis could hear the priests' chants echoing down the twisted corridors of the pyramid. To send Raman's soul to the gods, the priests would chant for the next three months.

Isis felt an icy chill roll down her back as she and Khufu approached the stone mummy case. Scenes of Raman as a baby flashed through her mind. She tried to fight back the tears, but a sob escaped her throat.

She waited as servants slid the heavy coffin lid off. Then she followed Khufu to the side of the case. She couldn't hold back the tears. They rolled down her face as she stared at the mummy, its arms still crossed tightly over its chest.

"Raman . . . Raman . . ." She whispered his name.

She and Khufu both let out screams as the mummy uncrossed its arms and sat up straight.

RAMAN LIVES!

Khufu uttered a bleating cry that sounded like a goat in pain. His knees folded, and he began to collapse. Isis caught him before he hit the hard floor.

Hot tears covered her eyes, turning everything before her into a blur. But she could see Raman twist in his mummy case and turn to her.

"Alive!" she choked out. "You're alive!"

She steadied Khufu on his feet and dove to the side of the case. Raman reached out a bandaged hand and smoothed his mother's cheek. She wrapped an arm around his neck and they remained this way, hugging for a long time.

Still breathing hard, Khufu began to revive. He stepped up beside Isis and gazed wide-eyed at the living mummy. "Vathor," he murmured.

Isis took a step back and turned to him. "What did you say? Khufu, this is a miracle! A miracle of the gods!"

"It's not a miracle," the old advisor replied. "It is the magic of the sorcerer Vathor. His spells are weak. They took some time. But they finally worked, and Raman is alive."

"Too late," the mummy whispered.

The sound of his words sent another chill down Isis's back. Her whole body shuddered. "You can speak, my son!"

"Too late," Raman repeated.

"The amulet," Khufu said. "Raman, do you know where it is?"

Raman shook his head.

"You do not know who took the amulet?"

The mummy shook his head again. "Too late for me," he repeated. "I am back to life, trapped in this costume of cloth and tar."

"But you are alive!" Isis declared, wiping more tears from her cheeks.

"Too late. Too late." Raman's voice came out like a whisper of air. He leaned toward Khufu. "You must bring Vathor to me. I will thank him for his magical skill."

Khufu bowed to the mummy. "We will do this, my king. We will bring Vathor to the palace to see you."

But this was easier said than done.

Servants brought the mummy case to the palace. It was placed in Raman's bedchamber to make him feel comfortable and at home.

Raman tried to talk to his brother and sister. But they were afraid of him now. They huddled at the door, too frightened to enter his room.

He walked stiffly and painfully. He spent most of the day lying in his coffin, staring up at the high ceiling.

"Too late . . ." he muttered often. "Too late."

Servants were sent to bring Vathor to the palace. But they reported he could not be found.

Finally, Maliki, assistant to the great wizard, came to explain. Maliki bowed to Isis and Khufu. Raman watched, sitting up in his case, placed next to the wall.

"Where is your master, Vathor?" Khufu demanded.

Maliki bowed again. He was a young man, no older than twenty. His face was pale, and his eyes blinked nervously. His legs shook, making his robe tremble.

"Vathor has d-disappeared," he stammered.

Khufu narrowed his eyes at Maliki. "Disappeared? Please explain."

The young man swallowed so hard, he made a

gulping sound. He took a breath. "My master, Vathor, is no longer here," he said finally. "He has used his time-travel powers."

"His *what*?" Isis cried.

"His time-travel powers," the young man repeated. "Vathor has used his powers to travel in time." His voice quivered. "My master has sent himself into the future."

Isis and Khufu stared at each other, trying to understand what Maliki had explained.

From his case against the wall, Raman was the first to speak. "Escaped," he rasped in a hoarse whisper.

Maliki uttered a frightened cry. "The mummy? It speaks?" he cried. He stumbled backward.

"Vathor brought Raman back to life," Khufu explained to him.

"Before he fled to the future," Isis added.

"The amulet," Raman said. "Vathor escaped to the future with my Osiris amulet."

Maliki uttered another frightened cry. "Please—do not blame me. I only bring you the news of Vathor's disappearance. I had no part in it."

Isis saw how terrified the young man was. He was trembling so hard, he could barely stand.

"We do not blame you," she said. "If Vathor has traveled to the future . . ."

"I must follow him there," Raman growled. "I will never rest until the amulet hangs safely around my neck once again."

PART THREE

Back at the Museum

Present Day

POSSESSED

"Ohhh, somebody help me!" I choked out. "Help! I'm being pulled . . . An invisible force . . . it's pulling me into the mummy case!"

Of course, there was no one around to hear my cries.

I had sneaked away from my class. And crept into the Egyptian Room, which was roped off. Closed.

But I was desperate. Desperate to see a real mummy. To get close to it. To smell it. To take some videos I could study later. And now something terrible was happening to me.

Jayden had begged me to come back to our class. He said we could return to see the mummy another day.

You should have listened to Jayden, I thought, as I struggled against the force.

But I was stubborn. Stubborn and desperate.

I'm sure you can understand. A real mummy! Who

gets to see a real mummy? Seeing the ancient mummy of the Boy King had meant everything to me.

But now, I froze in panic, open-mouthed. Fighting the force that was pulling me down. Fighting the pulsing vibrations that rocked my head.

The sour odor of the ancient cloth and tar filled my nostrils. My eyes blurred.

I tried to pull away.

But the more I fought back, the harder I was tugged down.

I struggled to raise my head. But I wasn't strong enough to fight the invisible magnet. My face touched the mummy's face. I felt the scratch of the ancient cloth on my forehead.

The force pressed against me . . . then yanked me . . . forcing me against the mummy.

"Help me!" I cried.

Can't somebody help me?

Why is this happening?

Then darkness washed over me, and my frantic thoughts ended.

It was as if I had suddenly fallen asleep.

Did I faint from my panic?

I don't know how long it lasted.

I woke sometime later. Blinking my eyes, I raised my head.

It took me a while to realize I was lying facedown on top of the mummy. A gasp escaped my throat as I pressed my hands against the sides of the mummy case.

Summoning all my strength, I pushed hard . . . pushed myself up. I could feel hot sweat on my forehead as I twisted and lowered a leg over the side of the case.

My whole body shuddered. I still had the putrid aroma of ancient decay in my nostrils. I could still feel the rough scratch of the mummy's bandages on my face.

With a hard tug, I slid over the side of the case and landed on my feet.

The floor tilted up and then down. The room spun in front of my eyes.

I grabbed the side of the case to steady myself. I tried to blink away my dizziness.

And then I heard a voice inside my head. Not my voice. A hoarse, whispery voice. It was soft but I could hear it clearly.

"Do not be afraid," the voice said. *"I am Raman the Boy King. I have taken possession of your mind. I have taken over your brain because I need your help."*

17

HAPPY SILVERMAN MEETS THE MUMMY

"No! No way! No!" I cried.

I shut my eyes and sat down on the floor.

I am imagining this, I told myself.

I'm hearing that voice because I got too excited about the mummy. I got too close to it.

Maybe I'm dreaming.

I shook my head hard, trying to shake the dream away. "Wake up, Happy," I said out loud. "Wake up."

But I was awake. I knew it. I could still hear the harsh, rasping whispered words.

"I am Raman the Boy King." That's what I heard. From inside my head.

I opened my eyes and glanced at the sign on the wall behind the mummy case. I read the name in large black type on the sign: RAMAN THE BOY KING.

With a shudder, I climbed to my feet. I took a deep

breath. "I have to get out of here," I said to myself. "I have to find my class."

And then the voice rattled in my head again. I felt a rumble in my ears. Then the harsh whisper.

"Do not be afraid. I mean you no harm."

"Where are you? Why are you talking to me?" The words tumbled from my mouth.

"I am Raman, and I need your help. You will help me find the amulet."

Amulet?

What was he talking about? Was I totally losing it?

I pressed my hands against my ears. I thought maybe I could shut the voice out. "Go away!" I shouted. "Go away! I know you're not real!"

"I have come a long way. Will you help me?" The words were soft but clear.

I lowered my hands. "Are you really in my mind?" I demanded. "Did you hypnotize me or something?"

"Hypnotize?" the voice repeated. *"That is not a word I know."*

"Please—go away," I said in a trembling voice. "Please—"

"I speak the truth. I am Raman the Boy King. I have

traveled many miles and thousands of years. The amulet brought me here. It calls to me. The amulet is near."

I tried to swallow. My mouth was as dry as cotton. Raman's words inside my brain made my ears hum.

"You—you are looking for an amulet?" I stammered. "Is that like a medallion or something?"

"The amulet of Osiris holds powerful magic," Raman's voice said. *"It has sent for me, its proper owner. Its power has allowed me to travel here. To enter your mind. I need to be close to the amulet to reclaim it."*

"But—why me?" I said.

"You will take me to it," the voice replied. *"The amulet is nearby. You will help me find it."*

"I—I can't," I stammered. "I'm too busy at school. Besides, I'm just a kid. You need an adult, someone who can get around town. Someone who knows what an amulet is."

Raman deepened his voice. *"You anger me,"* he boomed.

"Sorry. But you have to leave now," I said.

And then I uttered a shrill howl and grabbed my head as it exploded in pain. Bright red and yellow streaks flamed in front of my eyes.

I gripped my head in both hands, pressing hard, trying to force the throbbing pain away.

"*I can hurt you,*" Raman growled, so loud the words made my eyes water. "*I can hurt you if you anger me.*"

"But—but—" I sputtered. "I'd like to help you, but my parents wouldn't like it if—"

"*I have a better idea,*" Raman said. "*Since you do not wish to cooperate.*"

"A better idea?" I asked.

"*I will leave your mind here inside the mummy,*" Raman said. "*And I will take your body to go find the stolen amulet.*"

"No!" I cried. "Leave me inside the mummy? No way!" A wave of panic shook my whole body.

"*You will rest quietly,*" Raman said. "*Your mind will be at peace.*"

"No! No! No!" I cried. "I don't want to be a mummy."

"*It seems to be the best plan,*" Raman replied.

"No. Please—" I begged. I gazed down at the ragged mummy, so small, so smelly and old. The tar-stained rags of cloth . . . the small dips where the eyes used to be. "Please!"

I tensed my muscles and started to walk away. But Raman spun me around. He was controlling me now, controlling my legs. Forcing me back to the mummy case.

"Please—" my voice spilled out, high and shrill.

"*Rest now,*" his voice whispered inside my head. "*Rest easy.*"

I tried to fight the powerful force that seemed to be moving my mind, but I wasn't strong enough. The pulsing vibrations swept over me again. The room darkened.

I felt as if I was falling . . . falling onto the mummy.

Beat . . . beat . . . beat . . .

That was my heart. Beating in rhythm to the vibrations washing over me, trapping me, swallowing me.

I shut my eyes.

And when I opened them, I was staring up at the ceiling.

Unable to move my arms . . . my legs. Unable to turn my head.

Wrapped tightly in the putrid bandages. My arms crossed heavily over my chest.

I was inside the mummy now.

I WAS the mummy!

18

CAN HAPPY KEEP A SECRET?

My brain inside the mummy. Yes. I still had my mind. I could still think like me. I *was* me without my body.

I was trapped, a prisoner inside these ancient tar-stained rags. But somehow, I was alive. I was still Happy Silverman.

The bandages felt tight around my head. A narrow opening allowed me to see the ceiling. But could I make a sound? Could I speak?

I tried.

And uttered a croak, a choking sound.

And then I found my voice. "Wait!" I cried. "Raman? Are you still here? Wait!"

Silence.

I waited. Waited.

Then I called out again. "Raman?"

I heard footsteps, and then a face peered over the

side of the mummy case. *My* face. My face stared down at me. "What do you want?"

"D-don't leave me here," I stammered. "You need me."

My face blinked. "Need you?" Raman said in my voice. "Why do I need you?"

"Because you don't know anything," I said. My mind was spinning. I was thinking fast. "You don't know the town. You don't know my class. My friends. You don't know anyone."

He gazed down at me. He didn't reply.

"You don't know where I live," I said. "Where will you go at night? Where will you stay? You don't know what a school bus is. Or a car. Or *anything*."

He still didn't speak.

"You don't know *anything*!" I said again. "Everything has changed since you were alive. Listen to me, Raman. It's like you landed on a different planet."

"Planet?" he said finally. He scratched my head. "Planet*?*"

"You need me as a guide," I told him. "You want to find your amulet? You can't do it without my help."

He gazed down at me for another long moment. I could see he was thinking hard. Finally, he nodded. "You promise you will help me if I return you to your body?"

"I promise," I said. "I'm excited to help a king. An ancient king."

"I never lived to be ancient," he murmured. He lowered his eyes sadly. "I was murdered. Then a thief stole my amulet and escaped with it."

He gripped the side of the mummy case. "But I know where the thief is!" he exclaimed. "He is here."

"I—I can help you," I said. "I will search for him with you."

Was he going to let me out of this mummy and back into my body?

"I will not succeed if the thief knows I have followed him here," Raman said. "If I return you to your body . . . if I allow you to help me, you must keep me a secret. You must not let anyone know I am here."

"I'll keep your secret," I said. "I swear."

I'd swear *anything* to be released from this mummy! *Please. Please.*

If I could have crossed these mummy fingers, I would have had them all crossed.

"You must act as usual," Raman said. "You cannot give anyone a hint that I am here."

"I promise," I said. "No one will be able to guess."

He thought about it for another moment. Then I felt the vibrations start again, down the entire mummy body.

The room appeared to shake. Red and yellow smears of color clouded my eyes. And then I felt myself lifted . . . lifted from the mummy . . . lifted into midair.

I blinked several times. I swallowed.

Back. I was back in my body.

I clapped my hands. I jumped up and down a few times. Just testing.

Yes. Everything was working.

I gazed down at the mummy in the case. Had I really been inside that ancient thing?

"I have to get back to my class," I told Raman. "If I don't hurry, I'll be in major trouble."

I turned and started to walk out of the Egyptian Room.

"Remember to act as usual," he said. *"Do not allow anyone to guess our secret."*

"No worries," I told him.

I found Mr. Horvat and my class in the front lobby, preparing to leave the museum. Horvat came walking up to me. "I knew where you were, Happy," he said. "I knew it was important to you. So I decided to leave you there, even though the room was closed."

"Thank you," I said.

"I hope you found it interesting," he said.

I nodded. "Oh, for sure. It was *very* interesting."

He turned to the exit and started to lead the way to the school bus.

Abby and Jayden came hurrying up to me. "Did you get lost?" Abby said.

Jayden answered for me. "He snuck into the Egyptian Room."

Abby squinted at me. "Hey," she said, "there's something different about you."

Jayden studied me, too. "Yeah, she's right," he said. "What is it, Happy? What's different about you?"

"I got too close to the mummy," I said. "And now Raman the Boy King is inside my head."

19

"WHY AREN'T YOU SMILING?"

Why did I blurt that out? I guess it was just too much to keep inside.

Abby and Jayden both laughed.

"Weirdo," Abby said. "I said you looked different because you weren't smiling. You are always smiling, Happy."

"You are not a good keeper of secrets," Raman said in my mind. *"Of course, they do not believe you."*

I felt a shock of pain at my temples. I groaned and tried to rub it away with both hands.

"Do not try to convince them," Raman said. *"I can hurt you. You must obey me. I am right inside your head, and I can cause you much pain."*

"So? Why aren't you smiling?" Abby demanded.

"I've got stuff on my mind," I said.

She squinted at me. "Wasn't it exciting to see the mummy?"

"*Too* exciting," I answered.

I climbed onto the school bus and took a seat near the back. The ride to school seemed to take forever. I gazed out the window, and Raman gasped and uttered cries of surprise at everything he saw.

"Everything in the world has changed," he said. *"The carriage moves without anyone carrying it on their shoulders."*

"It's been thousands of years," I told him. "Things have changed a lot."

Lila Franklin, who was sitting in the row ahead of me, turned her head. "Happy, are you talking to yourself?"

"Yes," I said.

She stared at me for another few seconds, then turned back.

"I am amazed and confused by everything I see," Raman said. *"But I will stop talking about how much all this surprises me. I am here only to get my amulet back. Not to study this new world."*

"That's good," I replied.

"What's good?" Lila asked from the seat in front of me.

"Everything," I replied.

What am I going to do? I asked myself. *There isn't room for two of us in my mind. How am I going to survive this?*

I decided the best thing to do was help Raman find the amulet as quickly as I could. I had to obey him and do everything in my power to help him.

The sooner he had his amulet back, the sooner he would return to his place inside the mummy.

When I finally calmed down, I realized having an ancient Egyptian king inside my head was totally exciting and unbelievable. But would I ever be able to tell anyone about it? Would anyone ever believe me?

I turned and saw that Mr. Horvat had walked to my seat. He was standing over me, studying me.

"Happy," he said, "you got to spend a lot of time with the mummy."

I nodded. "For sure."

His eyes locked on mine. "I've read about Raman the Boy King," he said. "There are many stories about him. They say he was a good ruler for such a young king."

"Really?" I said. I didn't know how to answer him, and I knew Raman was listening.

"What was it like to see him?" Horvat asked.

"Uh . . . exciting," I said.

The bus bounced. Horvat grabbed the back of my seat. "Maybe you should write a report about Raman," he said. "Since you've seen him close-up."

"Okay," I said. "I'll do it."

Why was he staring so hard at me?

Did he know something? Had he guessed what had happened to me?

That was impossible, right?

WE HAVE TO DEFEAT A WIZARD

The bus dropped us off in the school parking lot. I walked home from there.

Raman was silent the whole way. He must have been amazed. I knew he had never seen houses or cars before.

I thought Raman would feel at home in my room since I have the big LEGO pyramid in the center of the floor. I dropped down onto the edge of my bed and waited for him to say something about it.

"I am receiving powerful signals from the amulet," he said. *"It is calling to me from nearby."*

"Good," I said. "Maybe it will be easy to find." I pointed to the pile of yellow LEGOs. "Don't you like my pyramid? It took my friends and me months to build."

"But it will not stand up in a sandstorm," the voice said. *"What building blocks did you use? You must use the heaviest stone bricks."*

"It's made out of LEGOs. Plastic," I told him.

"Plastic? Is that a new invention? Where is the pyramid entrance? It must face the river. And the tomb must be hidden deep in the chambers. What tiny person is buried in this pyramid?"

"It's just a toy," I said. "A model."

"We must go now in search of the amulet," Raman said. "We must hurry before Vathor senses that I have followed him here."

"Vathor?" I said. "Who is Vathor?"

"Happy?" Mom shouted from downstairs. "Who are you talking to?"

"Uh . . . I'm on the phone with Jayden," I called down to her. I don't like lying to Mom. But I didn't think explaining that I was talking to a voice in my head was a good idea.

"Vathor is the wizard who stole the amulet," Raman said. "Then he used its time-travel magic to escape from our land and our time."

"He escaped to my town?" I said. "How do you know he is here?"

"Because the amulet is alerting me. The amulet of Osiris brought me here. It belongs with me. We must go now. The signals are strong and so close."

I climbed to my feet. "It's not in this house," I said. "Vathor isn't here. Believe me."

"We will find him," Raman replied. *"And we will defeat him. We will leave now."*

My heart skipped a beat. I made a gulping sound. "Defeat him?"

"Vathor will not give up the amulet without a fight," Raman growled. *"But we will be ready for him."*

"We?" I choked out.

Mom stopped me at the bottom of the stairs. "Happy," she said, "where are you going? It's a school night, remember? Don't stay out too late."

"I'm going out to find an ancient Egyptian wizard," I answered.

"Well, you'd better take your poncho," she said. "It looks like rain."

21

"DON'T MAKE ME HURT YOU AGAIN"

I pulled on my rain poncho and headed out the front door. I waited for my eyes to adjust to the darkness. Clouds covered the moon and stars. The streetlamp at the curb was out.

I walked down the driveway to the sidewalk. In the house across the street, the neighbor's dog started to bark. An SUV rolled past, music pouring from its windows.

I glanced left and right. "Where should we walk?" I asked Raman. "Which way?"

"The amulet is calling me from the north," he replied.

I turned left and started to walk, my hands in my pockets. Our neighbor on the corner, Mr. Miller, waved to me from his driveway. He was hauling a large trash can to the curb.

"Has anyone new moved here?" Raman asked. *"Have you seen an old man here you never saw before?"*

"No," I said. "Is Vathor an old man?"

"He is. Have you seen anyone who might be an old wizard?"

"No," I said. "No old wizard."

At the corner, I started to cross the street. "Watch out!" a voice shouted. Two teenage girls on bikes whirred past. I leaped back.

I watched them pedal away. Then I crossed the street.

"Are we just going to walk and walk?" I asked. "I don't think any wizards live in my neighborhood. There's a creek a few blocks away, and the sidewalk ends."

"The amulet is calling to me," Raman replied. *"Its voice is growing stronger. We are going in the right direction."*

I sighed. "Okay. We'll keep walking. But I don't think we're going to find it this way."

"Turn here. Don't walk straight," Raman ordered.

I turned and started walking along Walnut Road, the side street. I felt a cold raindrop on my head. I should have brought an umbrella, I thought.

In the middle of the block, a voice called to me. "Hey, Happy. What are you doing here?"

I turned and saw Mr. Horvat. He was standing in his front yard, watering the lawn with a long garden hose.

I waved. "Hi, Mr. Horvat. I forgot you live here."

He turned off the hose and walked down the lawn to me. "Know why I'm watering the lawn?" He didn't give me a chance to answer. "I don't either. It rains every time I water the lawn."

I laughed. I didn't know what to say. It was weird running into my teacher like this.

"Where are you headed?" he asked.

I shrugged. "Just taking a walk," I said. Awkward. Why couldn't I think of a better story?

"Good exercise," he said. He smiled. "Still have mummies on the mind?"

Mummies on the mind?

Why did he say that?

Was he just talking? Or does he suspect something?

I heard a long rumble of thunder in the distance.

Then Raman spoke up. *"I'm getting signals. Very close. Ask him who lives in that house next door?"*

"Huh?" I turned and gazed at the house on the other side of a hedge. It looked old and run-down. A lot of shingles were missing. Some of the windowpanes were cracked. A broken gutter tilted down from the roof.

"Weird house next door," I said to Mr. Horvat.

He nodded. "It's empty," he said. "No one has lived there for years. Kids come and throw rocks at the windows." He sighed. "It's a shame. The house is just sitting there rotting."

"It's perfect!" Raman's voice exclaimed in my ears.

"It looks like a haunted house," I said.

Horvat grinned. "Maybe it *is* haunted. I do hear strange sounds coming from inside it late at night."

"Perfect," Raman repeated.

Raindrops pattered on the grass. "Better get inside," Horvat said. "And you'd better get home. See you in class tomorrow." Tugging the hose, he turned and strode back up the front lawn.

"Yes. I'd better get home," I said to Raman. I started back the way we had come.

"No!" Raman's cry rang in my ears.

I uttered a scream as pain exploded at my temples. I shut my eyes, waiting for it to fade.

"Into the old house," Raman ordered. *"My amulet is here. I know it is. It is calling to me with great power."*

"But—but—" I sputtered. "That house is scary. It might be dangerous. It might really be *haunted*."

"Into the house—now!" the voice boomed. *"Don't make me hurt you again."*

"WE ARE NOT ALONE"

The rain was coming down pretty hard as I stepped up to the front door of the old house. A jagged bolt of lightning flashed in the sky.

In the bright light, I could see cracks in the wooden door. A piece at the top had splintered off.

"It's probably locked," I told Raman.

Thunder boomed above my head. A gust of wind blew rain against my back.

"We must enter," Raman said. *"I am feeling the amulet's powerful voice."*

My hand trembled as I grabbed the brass doorknob.

"I—I don't want to do this," I stammered. "I have such a bad feeling."

"The amulet calls," Raman repeated. *"We cannot give in to your fear."*

I took a deep breath. Then I twisted the knob and

pushed. The door slid open easily. It made a creaking sound as it swung inside.

I peered into the dark entryway. Another flash of lightning lit up the living room. I saw a cluster of furniture covered in sheets. A couch maybe. Some chairs.

"Enter," Raman ordered. *"Do not delay."*

I had no choice. I stepped into the house and crept into the room. "Hey—!" I uttered a cry as something thumped over my shoes.

A rat?

Its feet tapped across the bare floor.

Rain pounded the dirty front windows. The floorboards squeaked as I took a few more steps.

I ducked as something fluttered over my head. It made a screeching sound. And then another creature made a flapping sound as it darted over me.

"Bats!" I cried. "The room is filled with bats."

Raman did not reply.

I swung back to the door. "We have to get out of here," I said. "The rats . . . the bats . . . We—we have to go—!"

"Silence!" Raman shouted. The cry made my ears rattle.

I held my breath. The only sound now was the rain

pelting the windows and the flapping wings of the bats swooping back and forth over my head.

"It is near . . . so near," Raman murmured.

And then a sound at the rear of the house made me jump. A creaking footstep. A door slamming.

Footsteps scraping heavily on a bare floor. Footsteps getting louder . . . coming closer.

"We are not alone," Raman said.

The words sent a chill down my spine.

And then a figure appeared out of the darkness.

A lightning bolt outside the window made the room bright as day again.

And I saw his white beard and his long gray coat. And his steely silver eyes peering out from under a hood that covered his head.

THE WIZARD?

"Vathor!"

Raman's cry throbbed in my head.

"Vathor! I knew he was here!"

The hooded man stopped halfway across the room from us. His silvery eyes narrowed underneath the hood. His hands were buried in the pockets of his long coat.

What was he about to do?

I had to hug myself to stop from shaking.

"Tell the old wizard I have come for what is mine!" Raman ordered.

I opened my mouth to speak, but no sound came out.

The old man stared at me. And then he said in a raspy croak: "Who are you? What are you doing here?"

"Are you . . . are you Vathor?" I stammered.

He scowled. "Who?"

"Vathor," I repeated, my voice cracking on the name.

He shook his head. The hood fell back, and I saw long, white hair hanging to his shoulders.

"What kind of name is *that*, kid?" he said.

"Do not let him fool you," came Raman's voice.

"What are you doing here?" the old man repeated. "Are you going to report me? Turn me in?"

I stared back at him. I didn't know how to answer those questions.

"Listen to me. My house burned down," he said. "I had no place to crash. So I've been here in this empty house. For a few weeks. You know. Till I can get myself together."

Was he telling the truth?

"You . . . you're not Vathor?" I choked out.

He snickered. "No. I'm Angelo. Angelo Fitzgerald." The silver eyes locked on mine. "Who are you?"

"Happy," I said.

"That's your name? Are you being funny?"

"No. That's what everyone calls me," I replied.

"Don't let the villain fool you!" Raman rasped. *"He has many wizard tricks. Demand the amulet. Demand it—now!"*

The old man took a few steps closer. I took a step back. Thunder crashed outside the window.

"Did you come in here to get out of the rain?" he asked.

"N-no," I stuttered. "You . . . you're a wizard. Right?"

His mouth dropped open. His front teeth were missing. "A wizard? You're being funny again?"

We stared at each other. I waited for him to answer.

He sighed. "Wish I was a wizard," he muttered. "I was a carpenter. But I injured my back. Haven't been able to get work. Then my house caught on fire . . ."

He rubbed his stubbled cheek with one hand. I think he was wiping away a tear. "Bad Luck is my middle name," he murmured.

"Are you listening to this?" I asked Raman. "I think I believe him."

Raman didn't reply.

The old man squinted at me. "Who are you talking to, kid?"

"Myself," I said.

A long silence. I waited for Raman to chime in.

Finally, he spoke in a whisper. *"This isn't Vathor. The signals from the amulet have weakened. The amulet is not in this house. This man is not Vathor."*

"I . . . I have to go now," I told the old man.

"You're not going to turn me in?"

I shook my head. "No. I won't tell anyone you're here. Promise."

"Thank you," he said. "I hope I can trust you."

"I promise," I said again. "The rain stopped, I think." I started to the door.

He hurried past me and blocked my path.

"I'm sorry, kid," he said. "But I can't let you leave."

I froze. A wave of panic shot down my body.

"I have to ask you a question first," he said.

"Question?" I replied.

He lowered his eyes. "I'm embarrassed to ask it. But . . . do you have any money on you? Anything at all?"

I reached into my jeans pocket. My fingers wrapped around two rolled-up dollar bills, the change from my lunch money. I held them out to him.

He snatched the money from my open hand. "Thank you. You're a good guy," he said, still avoiding my eyes. "Maybe I'll pay you back someday."

I didn't know what to say so I moved around him, hurried to the front door, and stepped outside. Rain was still coming down, but I didn't care. I wanted to get away from the old man and the creepy house.

I started to run. My shoes splashed through puddles,

and raindrops ran down my face. I felt like I wanted to run for miles.

I stopped at a corner to let a truck rumble past. Raman's voice rattled in my ears.

"I thought it was Vathor. I thought he was trying to fool us. Pretending to be an old man down on his luck. The amulet signals were strong. But the amulet wasn't in that house. He was telling the truth."

"How am I going to explain to my parents why I'm out here walking in the rain?" I said.

He ignored my question. *"We were close. I know we were. I could feel it. I don't know where we went wrong."*

"We'll keep looking," I said. I turned and started to jog up my front lawn. "I have to go to school tomorrow. But we can search after school."

"We have no choice," Raman said. *"The longer Vathor holds the amulet, the longer the world is in danger."*

"I promise," I told him. "Right after school. We'll search for him again."

"We'll search until we find him," Raman said. *"No matter how long it takes. Promise me."*

"Okay," I said. "Okay. I promise."

It didn't take long.

We found Vathor the next day.

24

THE WIZARD REVEALED

The next morning, Jayden appeared while Mom and I were having breakfast. He sat down beside me and took a slice of my toast.

He eats half of my breakfast almost every morning.

Mom started to stand up from her chair. "I'll make you some toast of your own," she told him.

"That's okay," Jayden said, reaching for my orange juice glass. "I already had breakfast." That's what he always says.

He finished the glass, then wiped his mouth with my napkin. "Happy, I texted you last night," he said. He had his eye on my Cheerios. "You didn't answer me."

"I . . . uh . . . went out," I said.

"Happy decided he needed a long walk in the rain," Mom said. "He came home soaking wet."

"Weird," Jayden said, studying me. "What was *that* about?"

I had to think fast. "Uh . . . well . . . it was a science experiment," I said. "For extra credit."

Mom is a scientist. She likes it whenever I get interested in science.

She took a sip from her coffee mug. "What was the experiment?" she asked.

"Well . . . I wanted to see how waterproof I am."

Jayden laughed. Mom scrunched up her face in a puzzled look. "That's for extra credit?" she asked.

"It was just step one," I said. "I need to do some more experiments."

It was so ridiculous, she didn't know what to say.

I ran up to my room and got my backpack. A few minutes later, Jayden and I were walking to school.

The sky was clear blue now. But the grass was still wet and the sidewalk had big puddles from last night's rain.

We waved to some kids from our class, rolling by in their dad's SUV. Jayden leaped over a wide puddle and just made it.

I was walking fast. I had a lot to think about.

He hurried to catch up to me. "What were you *really* doing out in the rain last night?" he demanded.

I wanted to tell him the truth. Like I said, I hate to lie. I wanted to tell him about how Raman the Boy King had invaded my mind in the museum. And how he was forcing me to hunt for the wizard who stole his magical amulet.

But, of course, there was no way Jayden would believe me if I told him the truth. And *no way* I wanted to face the throbbing pain Raman would send to my head if I dared to give away his secret.

I shrugged. "Just felt like walking," I told him.

"I started a new level of *Minecraft* on the PS5," he said. "You have to come over after school and see what I started to build."

"I think I'm busy," I replied.

"Huh? Busy?" He squinted at me.

"It's ancient Egypt stuff," I said. "I want to go online and check out some of the things I saw in the museum."

He slapped my shoulder. "They shouldn't have called you Happy. They should have called you Weirdo."

Mr. Horvat's Science class was our last class of the day. The classroom was already filled when Jayden and I arrived. Abby waved to us from her seat by the window.

Jayden and I took our places in the back row. I pulled my science text from my backpack and placed it on the desk in front of me.

The bell rang. No sign of Mr. Horvat. He was late.

Kids up front were laughing about something. Some were looking at their phones, even though we're not supposed to take our phones out except between classes.

I suddenly felt Raman stirring inside my brain. He muttered something I couldn't hear. And then his voice grew louder.

"Strange. Very strange."

I didn't reply. I didn't want kids to see me talking to myself. I waited for him to continue.

"The amulet," Raman said finally. *"I can feel its power. So strong. So close."*

"Are you sure?" I whispered, hoping no one saw me.

"Stronger than last night," he said. I could hear the excitement in his voice. *"Such a powerful signal. The amulet—it is very near."*

"I don't understand," I whispered. "Why would the amulet be here in my school?"

Jayden turned to me. "Did you say something to me?"

"No. Just clearing my throat," I said. I pretended to cough.

Mr. Horvat stepped into the room and walked to his desk. He wore a blue V-necked sweater over baggy khakis, and he carried a purple bag in one hand. It looked like one of the velvet bags my mom keeps her jewelry in.

"Hi, everyone," he said. He tucked the bag into a bottom desk drawer. "Sorry I'm late."

I felt a shock in my head that made me gasp. Pain raced from one temple to the other. And then another shockwave rattled my ears.

"The amulet!" Raman cried, so loud I had to shut my eyes. *"The amulet is in that bag! That man is Vathor!"*

HORVAT INSIDE OUT

"No way! That's my Science teacher," I said. I cupped my hands over my mouth so Jayden wouldn't see me talking to myself.

"The amulet is here. It is calling to me. How long has that man been your teacher? What does he call himself?" Raman cried. *"Quick—tell me!"*

"His name? It's Horvat," I said. "He's new to our school. He just started a few months ago."

Jayden was staring at me. I pretended to clear my throat again.

"We saw him last night, remember?" I told Raman. "His house was near the old abandoned house."

"That's why I was getting the strong signals," Raman said. *"The amulet was in his house. Not in the old house next door. In your teacher's house. We were so close."*

"But—but— Impossible. Mr. Horvat—" I started to protest.

"Horvat . . . Vathor . . ." Raman repeated. *"Horvat . . . Vathor . . ."*

I slapped my forehead when I suddenly realized.

If you spell *Horvat* inside out . . . If you move the last three letters in *Horvat* to the front . . . What do you get? You get *Vathor.*

"I don't believe it!" I exclaimed.

Everyone turned to me. I didn't mean to say it out loud.

Horvat stood up from his desk chair. "What don't you believe, Happy?" he asked.

"Uh . . . I don't believe it's Friday," I said. "This week—where did it go?"

Horvat studied me.

Could he tell that Raman was here? I wanted to ask Raman what he thought. But I couldn't talk to him with everyone in class watching me.

"Did you get caught in the rain last night?" Horvat asked me.

I nodded. "A little."

"Attack him!" Raman screamed in my head. So loud I had to shut my eyes. *"Don't talk about rain! ATTACK him! NOW! He put the amulet in his drawer! ATTACK!"*

Raman forced me out of my chair. I stumbled to my feet. "I can't—" I told him.

"You can't *what*?" Horvat demanded.

"I can't believe how hard it rained," I said, thinking fast.

Raman was screaming in my mind. I could barely hear the teacher.

Horvat squinted hard at me. "Happy, why are you standing up? Why do you look so troubled?"

"A bee," I answered. "I had a bee in my chair."

Does Horvat know?

Does he know I brought Raman with me? Does he know I know his true identity?

"*ATTACK him!*" Raman screamed. "*We will take my amulet and finish him for good!*"

He was forcing me forward. I grabbed the desk and fought to stay in place. "Not now!" I cried. "Not now!"

Several kids gasped at my outburst. Jayden laughed, as always.

The teacher took a few steps toward me, studying me as he walked. "Happy, do you feel okay?"

"N-no," I stammered. My mind was spinning. Raman was shouting and trying to force me to move. My head felt about to explode.

"I . . . have to see the nurse," I said.

I lurched toward the classroom door. But Horvat blocked my way. He put a hand on my shoulder and brought his face close to mine. "Happy," he whispered. "Is there something you want to tell me?"

26

"I KNOW WHAT YOU'RE DOING"

"N-no," I said. "I just don't feel well. I guess I shouldn't have stayed out in the rain."

I pushed past him and burst into the hall. I trotted toward the nurse's office. Glanced back to make sure he wasn't watching me. Then I turned a corner and stopped.

The halls were empty. Everyone was still in class. Across from me, I could hear the kids in the chorus singing. Loud laughter escaped from a room at the end of the hall.

"Raman, does he know you're here?" I demanded. "Can he sense you are with me?"

"I don't know," Raman replied. *"The amulet gives him powerful magic. It helped him conquer the art of time travel. But I don't know his mind powers."*

I tried to think about it, to make some kind of plan. But what kind of plan can you use when your Science teacher turns out to be an ancient Egyptian wizard?

"Why didn't you obey me?" Raman demanded. *"Why didn't you attack?"*

"You've got to be joking," I said, keeping my voice down. Voices traveled far in this empty hall. "Attack with what? Swing my backpack at him? Stab him with a permanent marker?"

"I don't know those words," Raman replied. *"I only know the amulet is crying out for me. It is in that desk, and we have to take it before Vathor escapes with it again."*

"We need a plan," I said. "Maybe we can grab it after school. You know. When the room is empty."

"I don't know if I can wait that long," Raman replied. *"If Vathor knows I am here . . ."* His voice trailed off.

"If we take the amulet," I said, thinking hard, "can we use it against Vathor? Can we use it to defeat him?"

"Yes. The magic of the amulet is much greater than that of the old wizard."

"Okay," I said. "We'll wait till after school. Then we'll take the amulet, and—"

I stopped because I heard footsteps. Hurried steps coming our way.

"Vathor!" Raman cried. The cry rattled in my ears.

I turned and saw I was standing near a supply closet

door. I dove for the door and grabbed the knob. Locked.

No time to run. No escape.

The thuds of the footsteps rang off the tile walls. My cousin Abby came running around the corner.

She stopped, surprised. "Happy," she said, "why are you out here?"

"Abby, why are *you* out here?" I asked. I breathed a sigh of relief.

"Mr. Horvat sent me to the nurse's office to see if you were okay," she answered.

"Yes," I said, nodding my head. "I'm okay. I just—"

"I know," she said. She narrowed her eyes at me and spoke in a whisper. "Happy, I know what you're doing."

27

AFTER SCHOOL, IT'S TERRIFYING

I gasped. "Abby—*what* did you just say?"

She rolled her eyes. "I said I know what you're doing."

How? How would Abby know anything?

Raman didn't speak. I waited for her to continue.

"I know you didn't study for the biped quiz," Abby said. "And you're out here acting sick so you don't have to take it this morning."

I couldn't help it. I burst out laughing.

She grabbed my sleeve. "Am I right?"

"No," I said, when I'd finished laughing. "I'm out here trying to make a plan to defeat an ancient Egyptian wizard."

"Ha. You're a riot," my cousin said. She gave me a hard shove. "Why can't you admit I'm right? You're supposed to be the science fanatic. Why are you trying to avoid the quiz?"

"Okay, okay. You're right," I said. "I messed up. I forgot to read the chapter."

She shoved me again. "I knew it," she said. "So what are you going to do? Go to the nurse and pretend to be sick? Or come back to class with me?"

I raised both hands in surrender. "I'll come take the quiz," I told her. "It's just one quiz. What's the big deal?"

The final bell rang.

Mr. Horvat closed his textbook and stood up from his desk. "Don't forget we have lab experiments next week," he said. "Be sure to bring your Science notebooks. See you all on Monday."

Everyone began talking at once. Stuffing things into their backpacks and hurrying to the door. I took my time. I knew I wasn't going anywhere.

Jayden stepped in front of me. "So? Let's go. Forget looking at the Egyptian stuff online. Come to my house," he said. "We'll play the PS5."

"I can't," I said. "Maybe tomorrow."

He frowned at me. "Why not?"

"I . . . promised my dad I'd do something," I replied.

"Huh? Do what?"

"I . . . don't remember," I said. "I just promised I'd do something with him. I have to go home so he can remind me."

He thought about it for a moment. "Okay. Later. Text me in the morning."

Out in the hall, kids were laughing and shouting. Locker doors slammed. Everyone stampeded to the exits to begin the weekend. A typical Friday afternoon.

I jammed my backpack into my locker. Then I headed to the boys' bathroom to wait till everyone had left.

"The amulet is calling to me," Raman said inside my head. *"We must act."*

"Be patient," I said. "The room will be empty soon. Everyone hurries away on Fridays. Even the teachers."

"I can feel it pulsing," he said.

Kids burst out laughing outside the bathroom door. Some girls were singing at the top of their lungs. Lockers clanged shut.

They're all happy and having fun, I thought. *Here I am, hiding in a bathroom, waiting to grab something an evil wizard stole thousands of years ago.*

"Raman," I said, "what will you do when we take the amulet?"

He was silent for a moment. Then he answered, *"I will use it to defeat Vathor. Then I will happily return with it to my resting place."*

"You will leave my mind and go back to your body in the museum?" I said.

"Yes. I will leave you with my heartfelt thanks. You are very brave."

I didn't feel brave. But I was glad to hear he planned to leave my mind.

I waited twenty minutes. The halls were silent now. The classroom would be empty. I started to push the door open. But I stopped.

Maybe I should wait longer.

I slid the door open a crack and peered out. I gazed up and down the hall. Empty. No one there. Someone had dropped a red baseball cap on the floor outside a classroom door. No other sign of life.

I took a deep breath to summon my courage. Raman said I was brave. But my heart began to flutter like a hummingbird in my chest, and my legs felt rubbery and weak as I crept into the hall.

What if Horvat is still in his classroom?

What if he catches me?

I wasn't brave. I was terrified.

But I had no idea just how terrified I was soon going to be.

A SURPRISE INTRUDER

My heartbeats were louder than my footsteps as I made my way down the empty hall. I could feel the blood pulsing at my temples.

Everything was telling me to turn around and go home. Run away.

But I knew Raman could hurt me if I failed him. And if I didn't help him . . . didn't take the amulet . . . would he ever leave my head?

I stopped a few feet outside the classroom.

I could feel Raman stir in my mind. I knew he had to be nervous, too.

"We are here," he said. *"I can feel it. We are so close."*

I took another deep breath. Then I leaned forward and poked my head into the classroom. The lights were still on. A metal blind rattled in the breeze from an open window.

No sign of Horvat. Not at his desk.

The Science supply closet door stood open. No sign of him in there.

I stepped into the doorway. My eyes swept the whole room. "All clear," I murmured to myself.

I walked into the room and closed the classroom door behind me.

"Do you still feel it? Are you still getting signals?" I asked.

"The amulet is here," Raman answered. *"Don't delay. Grab it."*

I hurried to the front of the room and stepped behind Horvat's desk. My hand trembled as I pulled open the bottom desk drawer. I fumbled around inside it. Papers . . . pens . . . a box of paper clips . . . no purple bag.

"I can't wait to see it again!" Raman cried inside my head. *"Its gold will dazzle you!"*

"I . . . I don't see the bag," I said. "He must have moved it."

"He had it in his house last night, and he brought it here today," Raman said.

"Maybe he took it home after school," I said. "Maybe he takes it wherever he goes."

"No," Raman replied. *"It's here. I can sense it."*

I rummaged through another desk drawer. Then another. No amulet.

"Are you still feeling powerful signals?" I asked.

"So close," he replied. *"The amulet is waiting for my hands to hold it."*

I turned to check out the bookshelf against the wall. It was filled with science textbooks, journals, and magazines. One shelf held a lifelike model of a human heart. The bottom shelf had several large glass jars, filled with a cloudy gray liquid.

"The supply closet," I murmured. "Maybe he put it there."

I glanced at the classroom door. My heart skipped a beat when I thought I saw a shadow move. But it was a shadow from the window.

No one there.

I took a second to catch my breath. Then I stepped into the closet and clicked on the ceiling light.

The shelves bulged with all kinds of science gear. Test tubes. Bunsen burners. Specimen jars.

I stepped up to the low wooden cabinet against the back wall.

"I can feel it!" Raman exclaimed. *"I can feel it strongly in here."*

I pulled open the top drawer. It was filled with computer photo paper.

The second drawer had a collection of wooden rulers.

"Hurry! Hurry!" Raman cried, so loud I thought my head might explode.

I slid open the bottom drawer of the little cabinet—

And there it was.

The purple bag. Why did Horvat move it here? Why didn't he take it back to his house?

I slid the amulet out and gasped as the gold flashed in front of my eyes. A five-sided amulet on a long, gold chain. Ancient hieroglyphs engraved on the front.

My hand trembled. The amulet was heavier than I'd imagined. My heart thudded in my chest. I raised the amulet high in both hands.

"Victory!" Raman's happy cry boomed in my ears. *"Victory! The amulet is returned! And Vathor is defeated!"*

Sunlight bounced off the golden object in my hands. It flashed brightly as if alive. I held it up and gazed at it.

"I can't believe it!" I cried out loud. "Me! Happy Silverman! I'm holding an amulet from ancient Egypt. An amulet that holds all kinds of magic!"

"Victory! Victory!" Raman cheered, making my head buzz.

"I . . . I have to take a selfie," I said. "I need to remember this moment. I need to have proof."

Gripping the amulet tightly in one hand, I reached into my jeans pocket for my phone.

But I froze when a voice shouted from the classroom doorway.

"I'll take it, Happy!"

I uttered a startled cry. Then I spun to the door and gasped.

"Give me the amulet, Happy. Give it to me—now."

"But . . . but . . ." I sputtered. "Jayden! What are you doing here?"

Jayden moved toward me quickly and stuck out a hand. "No questions. Hand it over. Now!"

29

A BOLT OF LIGHTNING

My mouth dropped open in shock. I tried to speak to him, but no sound came out.

Jayden stuck his hand in my face. "The amulet. Give it to me."

"No!" I finally found my voice. I staggered back, out of his reach. The amulet started to slip from my hand. I squeezed it harder and tucked it behind my back.

Jayden dove forward and tackled me around the waist. We both tumbled to the floor. He landed on top of me. The breath escaped my body in a loud whoosh.

The amulet hit the floor. We both scrambled for it, crawling over each other. I reached it first. Snatched it up and pressed it to my chest.

I climbed to my feet, and Jayden grabbed my shoulders and pushed me to the wall.

"Jayden—why?" I choked out. "Why?"

His face was drenched in sweat. His chest was

heaving up and down from his gulped breaths.

"Happy, listen to me," he rasped. "He—he's inside me. Inside my brain."

Jayden slammed my back against the wall. "Give me the amulet. He's *hurting* me."

"Who?" I cried. "Horvat?"

"He isn't really Horvat," Jayden replied. "He's an old wizard. He invaded my mind. He won't leave until I have the amulet."

"Vathor!" Raman spoke up.

"He realized this morning you were possessed by the Boy King," Jayden said. "He figured out why you were acting so weird. He moved it here to trap you. Vathor won't let you get away with the amulet. You have to give it to me. He—he'll explode my head or something. Please—!"

"Vathor cannot win!" Raman screamed in my ears. *"Use the amulet! Use it! You can destroy him!"*

"But my friend—" I started.

"You can save your friend! Use the power of the amulet!"

Gripping it in both hands, I raised the amulet to my chest. "I—I don't know how to use it!" I cried to Raman.

Jayden swiped a hand at it.

I swung it out of the way.

"Give it to me!" my friend screamed. "The wizard is hurting me!"

"Use it! You can use it!" Raman shouted.

Jayden shoved me hard against the wall. He grabbed the amulet with both hands and groaned as he struggled to pull it from me.

I tugged back with all my strength, and we both toppled to the floor again. I cried out as he jammed an elbow into my chest. I felt the amulet start to slip away.

With a cry, I tightened my grip on it. Jayden and I rolled around, wrestling for it. Grunting, groaning, we fought.

And then we both had it. We both gripped it in our hands. We tugged it back and forth. My arms ached. My hands throbbed.

I struggled to pull it from him.

And then the amulet let out a deafening *buzz*. It suddenly grew hot. So hot I cried out in pain and dropped it.

A streak of lightning—blinding white lightning— shot out from the amulet. It crackled and flamed. And surrounded me. Surrounded us both, circling us inside the buzzing white light.

I felt myself falling.

And then I didn't feel myself at all.

PART FOUR

Ancient Egypt

Thousands of Years Ago

30

VATHOR WINS

I gazed into a deep darkness. And then light slowly washed over me, like someone pulling a sheet away from my head. Blinking hard, I tried to focus.

It took me a while to realize I was lying on my back. I stared up at a ceiling of pale orange stone soaring above me. Murmured voices drifted through the room. They sounded hollow, as if I was in a very large space.

I tried to sit up. But pain crashed at my temples, and I lay back down.

I coughed and cleared my throat. I tried to speak. My eyes were still not focused. The ceiling seemed to be pulsing. I thought I could feel the hard floor tilt beneath me.

"Jayden?" I finally choked out. "Jayden? Are you here?"

No answer.

I raised my head again. I saw blue and orange curtains covering the walls. Furniture low to the floor. The room was vast. Stone columns rose to the ceiling all around. Pale sunlight washed in from tall windows high above my head.

No sign of Jayden.

"Where am I?" My voice bounced off the walls.

Fighting the pain, I managed to sit up. I braced my hands against the stone floor. I peered around the room. Several men and women in long robes and hoods were gathered at the far wall. Two gray cats sat side by side in a corner, their green eyes glowing.

Did the robed people see me?

They spoke in hushed tones. No one looked my way.

Am I invisible?

I pulled myself up to my knees. "I'm definitely not in school anymore," I told myself.

The amulet.

The word flashed into my mind.

I lowered my eyes to the floor and looked all around. The amulet was gone.

I stood up. I stretched, trying to loosen my tightened muscles. "Hello!" I shouted. "Can anyone hear me? Hello?"

Some of the robed people turned to look at me. One of the cats meowed.

"I can hear you!" a voice boomed.

I turned as a white-bearded old man in a black robe burst in front of me. His steel gray eyes narrowed as he looked at me. A thin smile formed beneath his beard.

He raised a shiny object in his hand and waved it in front of him. "Is this what you're looking for?"

The amulet.

"You are Vathor!" I exclaimed.

His grin grew wider.

"Wh-where are we?" I stammered.

"Back in time. Back in the palace of the gods."

"Jayden!" I said. "Where is my friend Jayden?"

"I left him in your school," the old wizard answered. "I have what I want. We don't need your friend here."

"Is he—is he okay?" I demanded.

Vathor's smile faded. "You don't need to worry about him," he growled. "You'll never see him again."

31

CATS

A cold shiver ran down my body. I stared at Vathor in horror.

Behind him, I heard cries of fright. The robed people were hurrying from the room. I was alone with him now, except for the two cats. They stood and began walking toward us, their tails curled in the air behind them.

Vathor raised the amulet. "Any last words?"

"Uh . . . well . . ." My mind whirred. What could I do? How could I save myself?

Sunlight from the high windows made the amulet sparkle.

I saw something move at the far wall. More cats had entered the vast chamber. Gray cats, moving silently, tails raised. They all had green eyes, glowing as bright as car headlights.

I counted a dozen cats. Maybe more. Heads lowered as if hunting prey, tails raised at attention.

"I see you admiring my servants," Vathor said. "Beautiful, aren't they?"

The cats formed a line across the floor as they advanced on us.

"Beautiful and hungry," Vathor said.

I took a stumbling step back. I was nearly at the wall. No way to escape.

Keeping their heads low, the cats silently moved closer, their eyes straight ahead, locked on me.

"I am here," said a voice in my head.

"Raman!" I cried out loud.

"I was stunned by the time travel," he said. *"But I am here. You must grab the amulet or the wizard will end you."*

"I . . . I can't," I replied.

"Has the Boy King come awake?" Vathor asked. A grin spread under his beard. "Good. Very good. He will perish with you. He will know that I am the new ruler of Egypt."

"Grab the amulet!" Raman cried inside my head.

But the cats surrounded me. They formed a circle around me. I couldn't move. They began to growl hungrily.

"This is goodbye," Vathor said, raising the amulet higher. "Goodbye, Raman. You see that my magic along with this amulet is more powerful than yours." He narrowed his eyes at me. "And goodbye to you, too, young man."

The cats growled and snarled hungrily. Their shrill cries rang off the stone walls until they were as loud as ambulance sirens.

I stood helpless, trembling. "Raman, help me!" I said.

"I cannot," he replied. *"I do not have the power for this . . ."*

Vathor rubbed his pointed beard. "I must feed my servants," he said, shouting over their cries. "Let me see. Shall I turn you into a mouse or a bird?"

A SNAKE

Vathor raised the amulet above his head and opened his mouth in a chant of strange words.

The cats' shrill screams were so loud, I covered my ears with both hands.

A mouse or a bird?

The words repeated in my mind as I pressed my hands to my ears. I felt a buzzing vibration in my head. I was about to shut my eyes when I saw something move against the far wall.

I squinted hard. Struggled to see clearly as the pulsing waves grew stronger in my head.

I saw a woman in a long, golden gown rushing across the floor toward us. She had a crown of green leaves resting on top of her flowing black hair.

Vathor didn't hear her until she was right behind him. He spun around and uttered a cry: "Isis!"

"Mother!" Raman's voice rumbled in my ears.

Vathor tried to spin away. But he wasn't fast enough.

Isis swiped the amulet from the old wizard's hands. Raised it above her head. And shouted a string of words.

"Noooooo!"

Vathor howled at the ceiling. He clasped his hands in front of him, as if begging her. The cats stopped their cries and scattered throughout the room.

Vathor dropped to his knees. His hands still clasped. Still begging.

As Isis continued her chant, Vathor sank to the floor.

I realized I wasn't breathing. I was watching in horror as the wizard's body melted . . . melted away.

In seconds, his robe collapsed to the floor. It spread out like a puddle. And then didn't move. Empty, I thought.

An empty robe.

But no. As I stared in amazement, a short black snake, about two feet long, wriggled out from inside the robe.

Vathor was a snake now.

Isis raised her sandal as if to stomp on him. But the snake slithered past her, making its way across the room. The cats watched it go, not interested in making the snake a meal.

Isis watched the snake until it disappeared out the

chamber door. Then she turned to me. "Vathor was a snake in my palace," she said. "Now he will end his days as a snake."

I opened my mouth to thank her for saving my life, but my throat was choked. I couldn't find my voice.

"You returned Vathor and the amulet," she said. She gripped the amulet tightly at her side. "Did you also return my son Raman?"

I nodded. "Y-yes," I stuttered. "Raman came with me from the future. He is inside my mind."

"Mother," he said in my ears. *"I am so happy to see you again. Thanks to Happy, the amulet is returned and back where it belongs."*

Of course, she couldn't hear him. I repeated his words to her.

"You are a brave young man," Isis said. "I shall see that my servants treat you to every luxury."

"Can I go home now?" I asked.

She didn't seem to hear my question.

"Raman," she said, looking at me but speaking to him. "We will return you to your tomb. You will be able to rest now with the amulet at your side."

She clapped her hands and several servants hurried into the chamber. "We will return my son to his place in the Pyramid of the Kings," she told them. "Prepare for the journey."

"After that?" I said. "After that, will you send me home?"

She tilted her head to one side as she squinted at me. "Return you home? To the future?"

"Yes," I said.

She sighed. "I'm so sorry. You cannot go back."

33

AN ACCIDENT IN THE TOMB

"Raman, help me!" I cried. "I can't stay here forever. I have to get home."

"There is no way," came the reply in my head.

"But *you* traveled to the future," I said. "You traveled to my time. You can use the amulet to send me back."

"I want you here," he replied. *"I want your bravery to help teach my brother and sister. Knowing you are here, I can go to my tomb and finally rest in peace."*

I stood there with my mouth hanging open. I suddenly felt dizzy. I leaned back against the wall and shut my eyes.

I'm trapped here, I thought. *Trapped in ancient Egypt.*

I'll never see my friends again . . . never see my family.

I felt a hand on my shoulder and opened my eyes to see Isis in front of me. "You will be treated as a prince," she said. "You will spend your days as a royal member of the palace."

I will spend my days as a prisoner here, I told myself.

For some reason, I thought of Jayden and his PS5 games. *I'll never have anything from the life I knew . . .*

"The carriage is ready," Isis said, turning to the chamber door. "We must return Raman to his resting place."

A short while later, six servants were carrying our carriage over the desert sands. This should have been a thrill for me. How amazing to be riding over ancient sands on our way to a towering pyramid.

But I couldn't enjoy it. I felt only dread at being trapped in this ancient kingdom for the rest of my life. Mom and Dad . . . Abby . . . Jayden . . . their faces flashed through my mind. I pictured my house . . . our school . . . the LEGO pyramid in my room.

The amazing scenery and the ancient people outside the bumping carriage meant nothing to me. Even when the mile-high Pyramid of the Kings rose over us, I felt only sad and sorry for myself.

Here I was, walking through dark, twisting pyramid tunnels and hidden chambers. A kid from the future, alive in this building from thousands of years ago. And I felt numb. No feelings . . . no excitement.

We walked miles along a twisting path, through dark chambers and low tunnels. Finally, we arrived at the mummy case. Servants raised torches, and I gazed into the flickering light.

How did the mummy get back here from the museum in my town? Raman must have used the power of the amulet to return it.

But I didn't really care about that. I didn't want to think about it. I didn't want to think about anything.

As I peered down at the mummy with its arms crossed over its chest, I felt Raman stir inside my mind.

"I must say farewell," he said. *"Farewell and thank you. You are honest and brave. I can only describe you as a hero."*

"Uh . . . glad to help," I muttered. I didn't know what to say.

I guess I'd come to think of him as a friend . . . a *very close* friend. But I also knew he had ruined my life.

I raised my hands to the sides of my face as my head began to buzz and vibrate.

"Farewell," came Raman's voice for the last time.

I suddenly felt lighter. The chamber appeared brighter. Everything appeared clear, as if a thin curtain had been lifted.

He was gone.

I gazed down at the mummy. Raman's resting place forever.

I turned when I felt a tap on my shoulder. Isis stood close beside me, her head veiled in black. She raised the amulet and handed it to me.

"You have earned the honor," she said. "Place the amulet beside my son in the burial case."

I don't want any honors. I just want to go home, I thought as I grasped the amulet.

Then it slid out of my hand.

It clattered to the stone floor.

"Sorry!" I cried. I bent over and picked it up. And smashed my head against the side of the stone mummy case.

"Hey—!" I uttered a cry as pain roared down my whole body.

And then everything went black.

34

SURPRISE AT SCHOOL

How long was I in darkness?

My eyes were shut when I felt someone shaking me by the shoulders.

I opened them and saw it was Abby. She was leaning over my desk. Blinking, struggling to focus, I saw that I was back in the classroom.

"Happy, what happened?" Abby demanded. "Did you fall asleep?"

I heard kids laughing. Everyone was staring at me.

"I—I—I—" I didn't know what to say.

I gazed around the room. I was back! I really was back. I wanted to jump out of my seat and do a happy dance.

"Welcome back to the living," a young woman said to me. She was perched on the edge of the desk at the front of the room. "I'm Miss Bethany," she said.

143

Abby returned to her desk. I shook my head, trying to wake myself up.

Did all that ancient Egypt stuff really happen to me?

"Mr. Horvat is no longer with the school," Miss Bethany said. "I'll be your Science teacher for the rest of the year."

Some kids muttered to one another. "Where did Mr. Horvat go?" someone asked.

Miss Bethany swept her long hair off her shoulders. "I really can't say. But I know you've been studying ancient Egypt. And I understand you all had a big disappointment."

Disappointment? What was she talking about?

"I heard that the Egyptian Room was closed when you visited the museum," she said. "Well, I have good news. The room has been opened up. And we will all go back there on Monday."

A grin spread over her face. "It's so awesome!" she exclaimed. "I hear they have a new mummy there. You'll get to see an actual mummy!"

ABOUT THE AUTHOR

R.L. Stine says he gets to scare people all over the world. So far, his books have sold more than 400 million copies, making him one of the most popular children's authors in history. The Goosebumps series has more than 150 titles and has inspired a TV series and two motion pictures. R.L. Stine himself is a character in the movies! He has also written the teen series Fear Street, which has been adapted into three Netflix movies, as well as other scary book series. His newest picture book for little kids, illustrated by Marc Brown, is titled *Why Did the Monster Cross the Road?* R.L. Stine lives in New York City with his wife, Jane, a former editor and publisher. You can learn more about him at rlstine.com.

Read on for a creepy sneak peek of
Say My Name! Say My Name!

PRESS PLAY

Before the fish started to talk . . . Before the hog monsters appeared . . . And before my whole world went weird and frightening . . . I wanted to go swimming.

I'm Cody Brachman. And if you knew me, you'd know how much I love to swim in the creek behind my house.

It was the warmest day of spring, and I was at my friend Sam's house. We were up in his room, and I was urging him to get into his swimsuit.

But Sam was giving me a hard time.

He begged me to stay at his house because he wanted to show off the new video game he had built.

Sam is a tech genius. He uses AI and invents his own games and does all the programming.

Someday, everyone in the world will be playing his games, and he might get too busy to go swimming in the creek with me. So I like to get our swims in while he's still not famous.

"I used AI to help program it," Sam said. "Cody, it's my most awesome game ever."

He raised his phone and snapped my photo.

"What's that for?" I asked.

He tapped at his phone for a while. "I have to get you into the game," he said. "You see, you and I are in the game. I already uploaded my picture and info about me. Now I'm uploading yours."

I glanced out the window. The glass appeared to be flaming from the bright sunlight.

"Sam, the water is calling me. Don't you hear it?" I said.

He put his hands behind his ears. "I don't hear it."

"Come on. Let's have a swim in the creek. Then we can come back and play the game." I grabbed his swim trunks from his dresser drawer, and pushed them into his arms. "Swim first," I said. "Game later."

"You don't understand," he said. "You've never seen anything like this game, and we're in it. Just watch."

He pressed Play.

The game started up.

And that's when my whole world started to go weird.

IN DEEP WATER

We walked to my house. I wanted to get my goggles.

Also, the creek starts to flow behind my backyard.

I found my goggles and folded a couple of towels in my arms.

We started out the back door. But my dad stopped us. "Wait. Where are you going?"

I rolled my eyes. "Since we're wearing swim trunks and carrying towels, three guesses," I said.

Dad says I have a smart mouth.

He may be right, but I don't know if having a smart mouth is good or bad.

He scratched the round patch at the top of his head where his scalp is showing. Dad says he's not going bald—his head is growing between the hairs. I guess that's his idea of a joke.

You can see why I'm the funny one in the family.

"I don't think swimming in the creek today is a good idea," he said.

Dad is always eager to tell me what isn't a good idea. He and I are very different. I'm bold, and he's timid. When he sits on the couch, he presses his back against it. He's afraid he might slide off the cushion.

Okay, okay. I made that up. But you get the idea.

"Sam and I swim in the creek all the time," I said. "What's the problem?"

Dad pointed out the back window. "We've had so much rain," he said. "The creek is overflowing its banks. The water is really high."

I groaned. "Dad, we're not going to drown in three feet of water," I said.

Sam rubbed his cheek. "Maybe your dad is right."

That made me laugh. "Sam," I said, "I'm twelve and my dad hasn't been right *yet*."

I was joking. But Dad just shook his head. I told you—no sense of humor.

Dad frowned. "Well, if you *do* go in, don't go past Deepwell Crossing. The creek can get deep and twisty there."

"We never go that far," Sam told him.

"The bottom drops out, and the current gets weird," Dad said. "And there are whirlpools. Some swimmers have had to be rescued." He shuddered. "Remember those kids who didn't make it?"

Dad remembers every time someone didn't make it. I don't think that's normal. But that's the way he thinks.

"Promise," I said. "No Deepwell Crossing." I raised my right hand to swear to it.

"Besides," Sam said, "we don't swim that much. We just wade in and try to catch fish in our hands."

"Is that fun?" Dad asked.

"It's good exercise," I said. "Builds up finger muscles. And, you know. Hand-eye coordination."

"It takes skill," Sam added. He shifted the small boat he was carrying to his other hand.

"What's that?" Dad finally noticed it.

"It's a remote-controlled sailboat," Sam said. He held it up. "I programmed it to do tricks in the water."

Dad stepped past us and started to the living room. "Okay, but be careful," he said. "The rocks on the creek bottom might be sharp."

"We'll step very lightly," I said.

"And take Ollie with you," Dad called from the hallway.

"We don't have a choice," I said. "Ollie follows us everywhere. Like a shadow." Ollie is a good dog, but he likes a lot of attention. Maybe all dogs do.

Ollie is pretty big, mostly German Shepherd with

some other dogs mixed in. He has a very long, very scratchy tongue. He'll lick your face off if you give him a chance.

Our house has a small, square backyard, and as I said, the creek flows right behind it.

As we walked to the creek, the tall grass that separates it from our yard was waving in a soft breeze. The spring air smelled fresh and sweet. Our sandals squished over the ground, still soft from all the rain.

Ollie tried to jump up and swipe the sailboat from Sam's hand. I guess he thought it was a dog toy. Sam swung it out of his reach, and we stepped into the tall grass.

"Wow, your dad was right!" Sam exclaimed. "Look. The water is up over the grass."

I gazed at the brown-green water. The creek was usually almost still. But today it was rushing past us, like a river.

Ollie leaped into the water and took big, splashing strokes, swimming in a wide circle. Sam and I followed the dog in, taking slow, careful steps. We weren't used to the strong current.

Goosebumps
HOUSE OF SHIVERS

#1: *Scariest. Book. Ever.*

#2: *Goblin Monday*

#3: *Night of the Living Mummy*

#4: *Say My Name! Say My Name!*

SCHOLASTIC.COM/GOOSEBUMPS

Goosebumps

The original bone-chilling series!

- ☐ NIGHT OF THE LIVING DUMMY
- ☐ DEEP TROUBLE
- ☐ MONSTER BLOOD
- ☐ THE HAUNTED MASK
- ☐ ONE DAY AT HORRORLAND
- ☐ THE CURSE OF THE MUMMY'S TOMB
- ☐ BE CAREFUL WHAT YOU WISH FOR
- ☐ SAY CHEESE AND DIE!
- ☐ THE HORROR AT CAMP JELLYJAM
- ☐ HOW I GOT MY SHRUNKEN HEAD
- ☐ THE WEREWOLF OF FEVER SWAMP
- ☐ A NIGHT IN TERROR TOWER
- ☐ WELCOME TO DEAD HOUSE
- ☐ WELCOME TO CAMP NIGHTMARE
- ☐ GHOST BEACH
- ☐ THE SCARECROW WALKS AT MIDNIGHT
- ☐ YOU CAN'T SCARE ME!
- ☐ RETURN OF THE MUMMY

- ☐ REVENGE OF THE LAWN GNOMES
- ☐ PHANTOM OF THE AUDITORIUM
- ☐ VAMPIRE BREATH
- ☐ STAY OUT OF THE BASEMENT
- ☐ A SHOCKER ON SHOCK STREET
- ☐ LET'S GET INVISIBLE!
- ☐ NIGHT OF THE LIVING DUMMY 2
- ☐ NIGHT OF THE LIVING DUMMY 3
- ☐ THE ABOMINABLE SNOWMAN OF PASADENA
- ☐ THE BLOB THAT ATE EVERYONE
- ☐ THE GHOST NEXT DOOR
- ☐ THE HAUNTED CAR
- ☐ ATTACK OF THE GRAVEYARD GHOULS
- ☐ PLEASE DON'T FEED THE VAMPIRE!
- ☐ THE HEADLESS GHOST
- ☐ THE HAUNTED MASK 2
- ☐ BRIDE OF THE LIVING DUMMY
- ☐ ATTACK OF THE JACK-O'-LANTERNS

SCHOLASTIC.COM/GOOSEBUMPS

Goosebumps

Read them all—if you dare!